STORYLINES

Conversational Skills Through Oral Histories

by
Priscilla Karant

Newbury House Publishers
A division of
Harper & Row, Publishers, Inc.

Cambridge, New York, Philadelphia, San Francisco, Washington, D.C.
London, Mexico City, São Paulo, Singapore, Sydney

Sponsoring Editor: Laurie Likoff
Text and Cover Design: Paul Kirouac/A Good Thing Inc.
Text Art: Ray Skibinski
Photos: Priscilla Karant (Chapters 3–5, 7–18), Ken Rice (Chapter 6)
Compositor: Com Com, A Division of Haddon Craftsmen Inc.
Printer and Binder: Malloy Lithographing Inc.

NEWBURY HOUSE PUBLISHERS
A division of Harper & Row, Publishers, Inc.

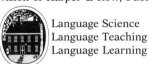 Language Science
Language Teaching
Language Learning

Storylines: Conversation Skills Through Oral Histories

Copyright © 1988 by Newbury House Publishers, Inc. A division of Harper & Row, Publishers, Inc. All rights reserved. Printed in the United States of America. No part of this book may be used or reproduced in any manner whatsoever without written permission, except in the case of brief quotations embodied in critical articles and reviews. For information address Harper & Row, Publishers, Inc., 10 East 53d Street, New York, NY 10022.

Library of Congress Cataloging in Publication Data

Karant, Priscilla, 1950–
    Storylines : conversation skills through oral histories / by Priscilla Karant.
      p.   cm.
    ISBN 0-06-632600-1
    1. English language—Textbooks for foreign speakers. 2. English language—Conversation and phrase books. 3. Conversation. 4. Oral history. I. Title.
PE1128.K36 1988
428.3'4—dc19   87-34729
                                           CIP

88 89 90 91 9 8 7 6 5 4 3 2 1

My love to
Arnaldo Ramos, Lynne Hale, Joshua Karant, Susie Karant, Mom, Dad, Fred Malkemes, Frank Ransom, Laraine Fletcher, and Nibo Biala for all their enthusiasm about Storylines.

My thanks to all the students who told me their stories and made this book possible.

Table of Contents

Introduction		xi
How to Use *Storylines*		xiii
Chapter 1	How to Be a Group Leader	1
Chapter 2	How to Use the Telephone	9
Chapter 3	*Yoko Hiyakawa*	19
	Think It Over:	Being Single, Marriage Pressures, Sex Discrimination
	Act It Out:	Asking for a Promotion, Greeting a Guest
	Call Up:	Inviting Someone to Dinner
Chapter 4	*Jaime Gonzalez*	25
	Think It Over:	Job Complaints, Dream Job, Acculturation Problems
	Act It Out:	Complaining
	Call Up:	Getting Information about an English Course
Chapter 5	*Jeong-Ja Kim*	29
	Think It Over:	Marrying for a Green Card, Living Together, Gambling
	Act It Out:	Giving Negative Opinions of a Person
	Call Up:	Getting Information about Changing a Visa

Chapter 6	*Gerard Le Pont*	33
	Think It Over:	Image of Foreigners, Marrying a Person with a Different Background
	Act It Out:	Giving Good News
	Call Up:	Giving Bad News
Chapter 7	*Dina Rubinov*	37
	Think It Over:	Changing Careers, Religious Persecution, Choosing a Religion
	Act It Out:	Making Excuses to a Teacher, Complimenting a Teacher
	Call Up:	Getting Information about an Advertised Job
Chapter 8	*Hector Rodriguez*	43
	Think It Over:	Illegal Aliens, Working Mothers
	Act It Out:	Expressing Anger
	Call Up:	Making Excuses for Being Late
Chapter 9	*May Chang*	49
	Think It Over:	Generation Gap, Dating Practices, Changing Traditions
	Act It Out:	Changing Someone's Mind
	Call Up:	Turning Down an Invitation
Chapter 10	*Taeb Omar*	55
	Think It Over:	Land of Opportunity, the Draft System, Draft Dodgers
	Act It Out:	Ordering at a Restaurant

	Call Up:	Getting Information about a Good Restaurant
Chapter 11	*Heidi Tobler*	59
	Think It Over:	Choosing a Profession, Privacy
	Act It Out:	Making Small Talk
	Call Up:	Confronting a Nosy Neighbor
Chapter 12	*Ali Fahrid*	63
	Think It Over:	Obeying Authorities, Making Judgments about People
	Act It Out:	Apologizing for a Mistake
	Call Up:	Getting Information about Hotels
Chapter 13	*Alejandra Maldonado*	69
	Think It Over:	Stereotypes, Apartment-Hunting, Attitudes toward Pets
	Act It Out:	Making Polite Requests
	Call Up:	Getting Information about an Advertised Apartment
Chapter 14	*Stanley Wolinski*	75
	Think It Over:	Learning English, Changing Job Status, Educational System
	Act It Out:	Teaching Your Language
	Call Up:	Giving Advice to a Tourist in Your Country
Chapter 15	*Marie Lionne*	81
	Think It Over:	Traits in a Mate, Brain Drain

	Act It Out:	Giving Compliments
	Call Up:	Saying Good-bye
Chapter 16	*Koji Watanabe*	87
	Think It Over:	Living Alone, Eating Habits, Obeying Signs
	Act It Out:	Borrowing Money
	Call Up:	Reporting a Theft
Chapter 17	*Kenny Lee*	93
	Think It Over:	Culture Shock on Returning Home, Humor
	Act It Out:	Telling a Joke
	Call Up:	Getting Information about Airline Flights
Chapter 18	*José Ojeda*	97
	Think It Over:	Trips, Services, Exchange Rates, Cost of Living
	Act It Out:	Saying Good-bye to Classmates, Greeting Old Friends
	Call Up:	Asking for Help
Appendix 1	Vocabulary List of Feelings	101
Appendix 2	Conversation Skills	103

    1. Asking Questions
    2. Asking Follow-Up Questions
    3. Hesitating
    4. Reporting
    5. Paraphrasing
    6. Rephrasing
    7. Listening Attentively
    8. Asking for Repetition
    9. Interrupting
    10. Returning to the Story
    11. Asking for Response
    12. Reacting Positively

13. Reacting Negatively
14. Giving Suggestions
15. Accepting Suggestions
16. Turning Down Suggestions
17. Ending a Conversation
18. Thanking
19. Responding to Thanks
20. Leaving

Oral Histories   111

Introduction

Storylines: Conversation Skills Through Oral Histories, is a conversation text for intermediate to advanced students of English as a second language who need practice in fluency. Its goal is total participation of a class by using small discussion groups.

The core of *Storylines* is the role-play of sixteen characters, familiar stories of foreigners living in the United States. An oral history of each character is included in Chapter 20. One student in each group studies the oral history and comes to class as the character of that story. The three other students in the group have not read the story; they interview the mystery student, with the goal of learning about the student's past, problems, and dreams. During the interview process, all conversation skills are practiced: asking questions, asking follow-up questions, rephrasing questions and answers, hesitating, paraphrasing, interrupting, asking for repetition, and asking for a response. All verb tenses are reviewed as students ask about the mystery student's present, past, and future.

The second stage of this group work is the response of the class to what the mystery student has revealed. Responses can take many forms: speculation, suggestions, praise, and disapproval.

Storylines was developed because of two problems commonly encountered in teaching conversation classes. The first is the silence of many students. The second is the inability of students to communicate personal feelings. With *Storylines,* these constraints are lifted, as students assume a different identity and work together in groups.

This book enables foreign students to practice basic communication skills in very natural settings while stimulating them to express their feelings.

The Level

Storylines has been used successfully with intermediate- to advanced-level students (TOEFL scores of 400 to 550). Low-intermediate students will be more challenged by some of the vocabulary and grammar structures. Encourage students to figure out the meaning of words from their context. Expressions can be memorized.

The Shy Student

These stories have been used with hundreds of students of different nationalities and temperaments. At first, the results were surprising; shyest students often became outspoken when it was their turn to be the mystery student. In my observation, working in small groups promotes self-confidence. Also, telling someone else's story tends to free shy students from their inhibitions. In fact, when students were videotaped while presenting their mystery characters, some of the best performers had been the quietest in class.

Why Use Mystery Students?

Whenever a visitor came to my classroom, an ideal situation for conversation was presented. Students were curious about who the person was, why he/she was there, and where he/she came from. In this natural situation, all levels of conversation skills were practiced, including listening, interacting, and responding. To make oral communications classes more real, I needed to have a constant stream of new faces. The mystery student fills the need to stimulate students to talk.

Why Use Stories of Foreigners?

America is a nation of immigrants. It is a place where thousands of young people from more than a hundred nations come to study. Many of the students of today become the workers of tomorrow. They are changing the face of America. What better way to help them adjust to a new society, even if they are here for only a short stay, than to discuss how others have adjusted to life in the United States?

The Cast of Characters

You will meet sixteen different people from different countries. Their stories are true. They have come to the United States for diverse reasons. Some have come as students, some as political refugees, some as temporary workers, some as permanent residents, and some as illegal aliens. They have come either alone, with their parents, or with their spouses. As culturally diverse as their backgrounds may appear, their stories are universal. Here to study or to work, they tell of their homesickness, their frustration with the language, their struggle to make friends, their visa problems, their difficulties at work, their "culture shock" on returning home, and their conflicts in love. Their problems are the human problems that anyone in a new country faces.

The chart on pages xiv–xv describes the characters and the goal of the activities within each chapter.

These oral histories are based on the experiences of real people. The names of the characters have been changed. Each story presents one person's point of view about a situation. These individuals are not representatives of their countries.

The oral histories should be used as springboards for discussion. If a story seems inappropriate, modify it to fit the needs of your students.

How to Use *Storylines*

Since the core of *Storylines* is group work, it is essential to work through Chapter 1, *How to Be a Group Leader.* Chapter 2 develops telephone skills, and should also be introduced during the first week of class. Complete guidelines and phrase lists for improving conversation skills are in Appendix 2, page 103. Words and phrases used in expressing feelings are in Appendix 1, page 101. This material is designed for use as part of each lesson before the mystery student is interviewed. The oral histories, printed at the back of the book, are on perforated pages. Some teachers may wish to collect them from the students' books at the beginning of the course, and then distribute them as each story comes up.

A sample lesson plan for the mystery student chapters, beginning with Chapter 3, is found on pages xvi–xviii.

Mystery Students and Chapter Activities

Name	Country	Age	Profession	Think It Over	Act It Out	Call Up	Chapter
Yoko Hiyakawa	Japan	27	Office worker, Japanese bank	Being Single, Marriage Pressures, Sex Discrimination	Asking for a Promotion, Greeting a Guest	Inviting Someone to Dinner	3
Jaime Gonzalez	Puerto Rico	48	Superintendent	Job Complaints, Dream Job, Acculturation Problems	Complaining	Getting Information about an English Course	4
Jeong-Ja Kim	Korea	23	Dancer, waitress	Marrying for a Green Card, Living Together, Gambling	Giving Negative Opinions of a Person	Getting Information about Changing a Visa	5
Gerard Le Pont	France	24	Hotel management student	Image of Foreigners, Marrying Person with a Different Background	Giving Good News	Giving Bad News	6
Dina Rubinov	Russia	43	Chemical engineer	Changing Careers, Religious Persecution, Choosing a Religion	Making Excuses to a Teacher, Complimenting a Teacher	Getting Information about an Advertised Job	7
Hector Rodriguez	Mexico	26	Janitor, parking lot attendant	Illegal Aliens, Working Mothers	Expressing Anger	Making Excuses for Being Late	8
May Chang	Taiwan	20	College student, math major	Generation Gap, Dating Practices, Changing Traditions	Changing Someone's Mind	Turning Down an Invitation	9
Taeb Omar	Afghanistan	28	Owner of a fast-food restaurant	Land of Opportunity, Draft System, Draft Dodgers	Ordering at a Restaurant	Getting Information about a Good Restaurant	10

Name	Country	Age	Profession	Think It Over	Act It Out	Call Up	Chapter
Heidi Tobler	Switzerland	22	Graduate student, art therapy	Choosing a Profession, Privacy	Making Small Talk with a Neighbor	Confronting a Nosy Neighbor	11
Ali Fahrid	Egypt	28	Security guard, dental student	Obeying Authorities, Making Judgments about People	Apologizing for a Mistake	Getting Information about Hotels	12
Alejandra Maldonado	Colómbia	22	Graduate student, social work	Stereotypes, Apartment-Hunting, Attitudes toward Pets	Making Polite Requests	Getting Information about an Advertised Apartment	13
Stanley Wolinski	Poland	40	Translator, doorman, taxi driver	Learning English, Changing of Job Status, Educational System	Teaching Your Language	Giving Advice to a Tourist in your Country	14
Marie Lionne	Haiti	19	College student, education major	Traits in a Mate, Brain Drain	Giving Compliments	Saying Good-bye	15
Koji Watanabe	Japan	27	Trainee at Japanese trading company	Living Alone, Eating Habits, Obeying Signs	Borrowing Money	Reporting a Theft	16
Kenny Lee	Hong Kong	21	Graduate student, business administration	Culture Shock on Return Home, Humor	Telling a Joke	Getting Information about Airline Flights	17
José Ojeda	Venezuela	32	Graduate student, counseling psychology	Trips, Services, Exchange Rates, Cost of Living	Saying Good-bye to Classmates, Greeting Old Friends	Asking for Help	18

Step One

> Ask all students to prepare for a class discussion of the Think It Over questions. Have them read the questions, analyze the problems presented, and form their opinions before coming to class.

Step Two

> Ask one-fourth of the students to read the oral history of the same mystery student. Try to assign them a person whose nationality is different from theirs. In other words, if the students are Chinese, do not assign a Chinese mystery student. Ask the students assigned to these sketches to think about the character before coming to class and develop their sketch as they see fit.

Step Three

> Have students respond to the Think It Over questions in class (thirty to forty minutes). This can be done in small groups (three or four students). Assign one student in each group to the role of leader; have the leader rotate every class. Leaders should elicit responses from their classmates as practiced in Chapter 1, "How to Be a Group Leader" (ten to twenty minutes). At the end of the session, the leader of each group should review the main points and report back to the class.

Step Four

> Have students use the Think It Over questions as the basis for a one-minute talk in front of the class (five to ten minutes). This assignment helps to build a student's confidence in speaking in front of groups. This speech should be prepared and rehearsed at home. Students should *not* use notes while speaking and should adhere strictly to the time limit. In class, you can focus on a student's individual problems in grammar and/or pronunciation.

Step Five

> Students can work on a particular conversation skill (fifteen to twenty-five minutes). Practice exercises are included for students who need extra work on a skill. Have students concentrate on using the new expressions during each interview session.

Step Six

One student of each group will have read the assigned oral history; in class, he or she becomes the mystery student (thirty to forty minutes). The other students in the group will interview the mystery student. All students will practice whatever skill(s) they have studied so far (such as questioning, paraphrasing, hesitating, or interrupting).

Step Seven

When the interview has been completed, have students read the oral history. Discuss the italicized expressions (five to fifteen minutes).

Step Eight

Assign students to the Act It Out role plays and have them spontaneously act out a situation. Then the class can discuss how a native English speaker might act in such a situation. These role plays can be done several times, with students switching partners until they feel comfortable in the situation (twenty to forty minutes).

Step Nine

Have students exchange phone numbers. Before students make a call, give hints on how to proceed (ten minutes). For example, two students can act out a specific call in front of the class. Everyone can comment on the performance. Sometimes a Call Up exercise will ask a student to call a real organization and not a classmate. If the suggestions given are not appropriate for your group of students, substitute some that are. Make sure students know how to use a telephone book to find what they need. Students should be encouraged to report back to the class on what happened when they made their phone calls (ten to twenty minutes).

Step Ten

Many of the exercises in *Storylines* can be used to teach writing skills. Here are some suggestions for writing assignments:

a response to the mystery student sketch;
answers to the Think It Over questions;

a script for the role plays;
an oral history of someone they know to create their own mystery student;
an autobiographical sketch;
a report on their telephone conversations;
a story about the mystery student ten years from now;
a letter giving advice to the mystery student.

Guidelines for Correcting in a Group Setting

1. Beware of overcorrection. You are interested in promoting fluency practice, so do not create an atmosphere that is inhibiting to students.
2. Emphasize one type of correction in each session. If you are working on asking questions, focus on making sure that students are using the correct word order and verb form.
3. If possible, have students self-correct. This forces students to think more about their errors. If this is not possible, see if anyone in the group can help. Teaching students to help themselves and others on their own is ideal.
4. Be sensitive to each student you are working with. Is the student highly sensitive to criticism? Try to compliment the student while pointing out errors. Is he/she the type who becomes defensive about being right? Encourage other students to help you. It can also be helpful to tape such students. Does the student speak so quickly that he/she pays no attention to the correction and just keeps on talking? If so, slow the student down and suggest writing out the correction.
5. Avoid correcting during a heated discussion. Instead, jot down the error you want to point out and wait for a break in the discussion.
6. Do make corrections. The most frequent student complaint is that teachers do not correct enough.

It takes time to feel out the students in a classroom and to understand what will work best for them. Just try to remain sensitive to the individual and to the situation.

CHAPTER 1

How to Be a Group Leader

Before you can be a group leader, you need to know your classmates' names. Also, you must learn to say your name clearly so that everyone can understand.

Exercise 1

Stand up and introduce yourself to the class. Remember to say your name slowly. If you have not understood someone's name, ask the person to repeat it slowly and/or spell it.

Example: Hello, my name is F******** Z********.
Other students: I'm sorry, I didn't catch your first (last) name.
Would you mind repeating it?
Would you say your name slowly, please?
Could you spell your first (last) name?

Once you have understood the student's name, you should repeat it.

Example: Oh! Franco. I'm very pleased (happy, glad) to meet you.

If a student has mispronounced your name, feel free to correct him/her.

Example: I'm afraid you have misunderstood me. My last name is Rhee, not Lee.
No, it's Arnaldo. You have to roll the "r."
No, it's Priscílla. The accent is on the second syllable.

If you prefer to be called by a nickname, this is how you introduce yourself:

Example: My name is William. But you can call me Bill.

My name is Ivan. But you can call me by my American name, John.

In American classrooms, students call each other by their first names.

Example: My name is Franco Zerlanger. But you can call me by my first name, Franco.

Exercise 2

Let's see how well you learned your classmates' names. Go to the front of the class and introduce three students to the teacher, one by one.

Example: I'd like to introduce you to a (very good) friend of mine.
I'd like you to meet Franco (a friend of mine).
Franco, this is Arnaldo.
Oh, Arnaldo! I'm so glad to meet you. I've heard so much about you.

Much of your work in class will be done in small groups. Each group will have a group leader. The job of group leader will rotate so that each student will have several chances to practice the important skills of leading a discussion.

Being a group leader means being sensitive to the needs of all the students in your group.

- You need to get shy students to talk.
- You need to get more talkative students to give others a chance to participate.
- You need to get fast talkers to slow down.
- You need to get the soft-spoken to speak up.
- You need to get the poor speakers to rephrase their thoughts.
- You need to get the student who wanders off the topic back on track.

- You need to calm down an overly excited student.
- You need to remain silent while others are talking.
- You need to sum up what has been said.

Exercise 3

With your classmates, think of ways you could handle the preceding situations. If you need help, refer to the expressions below.

1. For More Participation

There are several ways to elicit responses from your fellow students. The following are some questions you could ask.

- Sue says. . . . What do you think, Nibo?
- Do you all agree with Renko's idea about . . . ?
- Does anyone have anything else to add?
- Would you like to ask Naresh a question?
- We haven't heard from Arnaldo. What do you think about . . . ?
- Does everyone understand what Franco said?
- What do you think he meant?

Practice

In groups of four, discuss good ways to meet men/women. Whoever is doing the most talking should get the others to participate more. Use the expressions above.

2. For Wanderers

Sometimes a student may go off the topic. To get a wanderer back to the topic, you can say the following:

- Well, let's get back to the question.
- Let's return to what Laraine was saying.

Practice

In groups of four, discuss what you like (don't like) about the American foreign policy. One student should keep going off the topic.

Example: Oh, by the way, did I tell you about the movie I saw last night?

Use the expressions above to get the student back to the topic.

3. For Mumblers

Some students mumble. Mumbling is very frustrating to the other students who are trying to understand what is being said. To get a mumbler to speak up, you can say:

- ■ I'm afraid we can't quite hear (make out) what you said.
- ■ Would you mind speaking up?
- ■ Could you please speak a little louder?

4. For Fast Talkers

If a student is speaking too quickly, you can say:

- ■ We're having trouble following you.
- ■ Would you mind slowing down?

Practice

In groups of four, discuss your favorite movies. Tell why you like them. Anyone speaking too softly should be told to speak up. Anyone speaking too quickly should be told to slow down. Use the expressions above.

5. For Monopolizers

If someone is monopolizing the discussion, you can break in by saying:

- ■ Thank you very much for your comments.
- ■ Let's hear from someone else now.
- ■ Let's hear what the others have to say.

6. For the Impatient

If an impatient student is interrupting others too frequently, you can say:

- ■ Hold on! Let him (her) finish what he's (she's) saying.
- ■ Wait your turn, please!
- ■ Be patient! You'll get a chance to talk.

7. For the Overly Excited

If a student gets overly excited, you can say:

- Calm down! Relax!
- Let's hear everything he/she has to say before we interrupt him/her.

Practice

In groups of four, discuss your ambitions. One student should try to monopolize the conversation by not letting anyone else talk. The others should control him/her by using the preceding expressions.

8. For the Unclear Talkers

If a student is having a hard time expressing his/her ideas, encourage that person to reword his/her thoughts.

- I'm afraid we don't quite get your point.
- Would you mind rephrasing that?
- I'm not sure we've understood what you meant.
- What would you like to say? What was that?

Practice

In groups of four, discuss why studying English is important to you. If you have trouble understanding any of the students, use the expressions above.

9. For Summing Up

At the end of a discussion, you should review the main points made by other group members and be able to report back to the class on what was said. You can introduce summing up with these expressions:

- In brief, . . .
- In sum, . . .
- In general, . . .
- All in all, . . .
- Basically, . . .

Practice

In groups of four, discuss whether it is better to go to a coed school or to an all boys'/girls' school. At the end of the discussion, summarize your main point in one sentence. Use the expressions above.

Check Yourself

Work with a partner to determine what would be best to say if you were the group leader in the following situations. Write down as many expressions as you can think of for each problem.

YOU ARE THINKING: YOU SHOULD SAY:

1. I can't hear him. Is he really talking?

2. That one is a real windbag! When will he get to the point?

3. Gosh! That guy has been talking for ten minutes straight. Is he ever going to stop?

4. Is that English she's speaking? How am I supposed to understand that?

5. My goodness! She's talking as if she's in a race against time. When is she going to take a breath of air?

6. Is that woman asleep? I haven't seen her open her mouth once!

7. He looks as if he has something he wants to say. I'd better call on him.

8. I wonder what the rest of the class thinks about what he has just said.

YOU ARE THINKING:	YOU SHOULD SAY:
9. Oops! She's changing the topic. I'd better get her back on track.	
10. I wonder if everyone understood what he just said. It was pretty complicated.	
11. Oh, no! She's going to interrupt again. She just can't wait. I'd better stop her.	
12. I can't believe how excited he's getting. It looks like he wants to strangle the guy next to him. I'd better calm him down.	

CHAPTER 2

How to Use the Telephone

Throughout the semester, you will be making phone calls as part of your homework assignments. Translating what you would say in your language into English may sometimes sound rude or confusing to an American. Instead of translating, learn American telephone language to facilitate all your phone conversations.

Exercise

With your classmates, discuss what you would say on the telephone in the following situations.

1. Opening the conversation
2. Asking for identification
3. Identifying yourself
4. Asking someone to repeat what was said
5. Telling someone that you are too busy to talk
6. Telling the caller to hold on
7. Leaving a message
8. Ending a conversation
9. Leaving a message on an answering machine
10. Calling an operator for an overseas call
11. Calling the operator about telephone trouble

Now take a look at the following expressions and see how well you did.

1. Opening the Conversation

- Hello, may I please speak to Mrs. Ramos?
- Hello, could I please speak to Mr. Biala?
- Hello, I'd like to speak to Ms. Kim.
- Hello, is Joshua there?
- Hello, is Philip in?

2. Asking for Identification

- Who's calling, please?
- Who is this, please?

3. Identifying Yourself

- This is Mrs. Azia.
- This is Mr. Levy speaking.
- This is Ms. Kim calling.
- This is Esther.

Practice

1. Discuss the differences between these expressions. Which are more formal?
2. How would you start a conversation on the telephone with: a teacher, a boss, a classmate, an unknown person at an office?

4. Answering the Telephone When Someone Isn't In

- I'm sorry, but Ms. Teller isn't here right now. Would you like to leave a message?
- I'm sorry, but Ms. Langlieb just stepped away from her desk. Would you like to try again in a little while?
- I'm sorry, but Mr. Dubin is tied up at a meeting right now. Would you like to call back in an hour?
- I'm sorry, but Waheed is out to lunch right now. Is there any message?
- Oh, Lynne just went out to do the laundry. Do you want to leave a message?

5. When Someone Isn't Available

- What is a good time to reach her?
- When do you expect him?
- I'll call back later.
- I'll try later.
- Please tell Melinda to give me a call when she's free.
                                         as soon as possible.
                                         later on today.
- My name is Joshua Karant. That's K-A-R-A-N-T. (Say your name *slowly*. Spell your name *slowly*.)
- She can reach me at area code 615(pause) 562(pause)-2060. (Say each digit of a phone number individually. Say "oh," *not* zero.)

Practice

1. With a partner, try out these expressions. Pretend that you are calling the director of an English school, a teacher, a classmate, and a business partner.

6. Asking Someone to Repeat What Was Said

- I'm sorry (excuse me, pardon me), what did you say?
- Could you please slow down? I'm having trouble following you.
- Would you mind repeating that?
- How do you spell that?
- Would you mind spelling that?
- I didn't catch what you said.
- That was _____, wasn't it?
- Did you say _____?
- Was that _____?

Practice

1. Discuss the differences between these expressions. Which are more formal?
2. With a partner, try out these expressions. Pretend that you are calling:
   a. a classmate for the name and the address of his/her favorite restaurant.
   b. an employer for a job interview. Ask for directions to the office.

7. Telling the Caller to Hold On

- Hold on one moment, please.
- Just a second, I'll check.
- Just a moment, I'll see.

Practice

Which of these expressions is the most formal?

8. Too Busy to Talk

The Caller
- Is this a good time to call? I hope I'm not interrupting anything.
- Do you have a minute to talk?
- Are you free now?
- Can you talk now?

Response
- I'm in the middle of something. Can I call you back in a few minutes?
- I was just about to leave the house. Can I call you later?
- I'm on my way out. How about calling back in an hour?
- I'm tied up at the moment. When is a good time to catch you?
- Let me take down your number. I'll call you right back.

Practice

With a partner, try out these expressions. Pretend that you are calling:

1. a classmate for next week's assignment. It is around dinnertime and the person is in the middle of cooking dinner.
2. one of your teachers who is just about to leave the office to teach a class.
3. a business associate who has just received a call on another line. It's a very important call that must be taken now.
4. a friend who is watching a very exciting mystery movie on television and doesn't want to miss the end.

9. Ending a Conversation

The Caller
- Well, it's been good talking to you.
- I'd better let you go.
- Thanks for your time.

- I appreciate your help.
- I've really enjoyed talking to you.
- I hope to speak to you (hear from you) soon.
- Speak to you soon.

10. Ending a Conversation

The Person Being Called

- Well, thanks for calling.
- It was really good to hear from you.
- Give me a call if you have any more questions.
- Let me know if I can be of any more help.
- Feel free to call again.

Practice

1. Discuss the differences between these expressions. Which are more formal?
2. With a partner, try out these expressions. Pretend that you are calling:
   a. a classmate for information on what you missed in class when you were absent.
   b. a travel agent for information on a good spot for a one-week vacation.

11. Leaving a Message on an Answering Machine

Many people now have answering machines at home to receive messages while they are out. When you reach an answering machine, you will hear a recorded announcement like this: "Hello. You have reached the home of Mary and Philip Bedick. We are unable to come to the phone right now. Please leave a message when you hear the beep."

Here are some messages you can leave when you hear the beep:

- Hello, this is Carolyn. I'm sorry I missed you. Give me a call when you get home. My number is 657-7207.

More Formal

- Hello, this is Mr. Levy from Citibank. I'm calling about your mortgage loan application. I will be at the office until five o'clock. You can reach me at 598-3000, extension 391.

Practice

Write down the kind of announcement that you would want to have on your answering machine at home. Then, with two partners, practice calling one another. The person being called must read his/her recorded announcement, while the student calling must practice leaving a message.

12. Calling the Operator

- Can you give me the area code for San Francisco?
- What is the number for information in Manhattan?
- I'd like to make an overseas call to Caracas, Venezuela. The number is_____.
- I'd like to make a long-distance call and charge it to my home number.
- I'd like to make a collect call to area code (201) 737-8822. My name is Ramon Ramos.
- I'd like to make a person-to-person call to Mr. Park. The number is_____.

13. Calling the Operator about Telephone Trouble

- I just lost a quarter in this phone. Can you give me credit, please?
- I'm having trouble getting through to this number. Could you please check the line and dial it for me?
- I just called the wrong number. Can you give me credit, please?
- I was cut off in the middle of my call. Could you give me credit for the call?
- There was so much static on the line that I couldn't hear the other party. Could you give me credit for the call, please?

Practice

With a partner, try out these expressions. Pretend that you are calling the operator:

1. to get back money that you lost in a public phone.
2. to dial a number you are having difficulty getting.
3. to make a collect call (from your home phone).

Extra Practice

Make the following phone calls. Try to use some of the new expressions you have learned. Then, in groups of three, report back on what you have learned.

Call #1: Look through a local newspaper for a movie you are interested in seeing. Call the theater for the show times, the price of a ticket, the length of the film, and directions to the theater. If you receive a recording, just copy down any information that is given.

Call #2: Call the local (university) library. Find out the hours it is open. Find out if the library receives any newspapers from your country.

Call #3: Find out the number for the local newspaper. Check the prices for home delivery.

Check Yourself

Test yourself on how well you have learned telephone language. Choose the best response for the following situations. Circle the letters of the correct answers. Then check your answers. Discuss your answers with your teacher.

1. When I make a phone call, the first thing I should say is:
   a. Hello, who is this?
   b. Hello, I am Mr. Rice.
   c. Hello, may I please speak to Ms. Levine?
   d. Hello, I want to talk to Mrs. Fabrizi.
2. When I answer the phone and want to know who is calling, I should say:
   a. Who's there, please?
   b. Who is it, please?
   c. Who's calling, please?
3. When I tell someone my name, I should say:
   a. It's Esther.
   b. Esther is speaking.
   c. This is Esther.
   d. It's Esther calling.

4. When I don't understand something, I should say:
   a. Would you mind repeating that?
   b. Nothing, and pretend that I have understood.
5. When I am afraid that the person I am calling is too busy to talk, I should say:
   a. Nothing about that and just say what I wanted.
   b. Is this a good time to talk?
6. When I am too busy to talk, I should say:
   a. I'm busy. I can't talk.
   b. I'm afraid that I'm busy right now. Can I call you back in an hour?
7. When a caller asks for someone who isn't in, I should say:
   a. He's not here.
   b. I'm sorry, but she's not here right now. Would you like to leave a message?
8. If I lose some money in a pay telephone, I should:
   a. Forget about it.
   b. Call the operator and say, "Give me my money back."
   c. Call the operator and say, "I just lost a quarter in the phone booth. Can you give me credit, please?"
9. The correct way to say the number 598-3930 is:
   a. five-nine-eight (pause) thirty-nine-thirty
   b. five-nine-eight (pause) three-nine-three-oh
   c. five-nine-eight (pause) three-nine-three-zero
10. If I want to ask someone to spell something, I should say:
    a. How do you spell that?
    b. What? I didn't catch that.
    c. I'm sorry. I don't understand.
    d. Spell it.

Answers: 1c, 2c, 3c, 4a, 5b, 6b, 7b, 8c, 9b, 10a.

Final Practice

Exchange phone numbers with your classmates. Make the following phone calls to practice the new expressions you have learned. Then, in groups of three, report back on what happened when you called.

1. Call Mr. Quaintance. You are put on hold. You are then told he isn't in. Leave a message.
2. Call the operator to make an overseas call. Find out when the rates are the lowest.

3. Call your classmate for a mutual friend's name, address, and phone number. Use the expressions for repetition. End the call politely.
4. Call your classmate to talk about school. He/she is too busy to talk and wants to call you later. Arrange a convenient time to call back.

CHAPTER 3
Yoko Hiyakawa

1. Think It Over

Be prepared to express your opinions on these questions in class.

1. Do young people in your country feel pressure to get married? At what age is this pressure exerted? Who exerts this pressure? Describe a typical situation in which a single person is discouraged from remaining single. Is the pressure the same for a woman as for a man? Do you think that this pressure is healthy?
2. How is an unmarried thirty-five-year-old man viewed in your country? an unmarried thirty-five-year-old woman?
3. Have you ever been passed over for a job promotion or a school award because of your sex or nationality? Describe what happened.
4. If you were a boss, what criteria would you use for giving a promotion? Rate the items below in order of importance. Explain your answers.

   length of time in the job   social relationship with you
   age   appearance
   personality   skills
   educational background   race
   marital status   ethnic background
   sex

5. In April 1987, the United States Supreme Court ruled in favor of affirmative action, stating that it was proper for employers to use the race, sex, and ethnic background of a

qualified person as criteria for a promotion to make up for past discrimination. For example, if a black man and a white man with equal qualifications applied for the same position, it would be proper to give the job to the black man. How do you feel about this decision?

2. One-Minute Speech

Ask two students to give a brief talk in front of the class about any one of the questions above.

3. Conversation Skills

Asking Questions

Here are some questions that an American might ask a foreigner living in the United States. What other questions might you ask?

What's your name?
Where are you from?
Where were you born?
How long have you been in this country?
Where do you live now?
Why did you come to this country?
What kind of visa do you have?
Are you here with your family?
Are you married?
Do you have any children?
When will you return to your country?
Are you eager to return?
Would you prefer to stay here longer?
What do you do for a living?
What's your job like?
What do you enjoy about your job?
What would you like to be doing two years from now? ten years from now?
What are some of your favorite activities here?
What has surprised you about life in this country?
What kind of problems have you run up against here?

Practice

In small groups, practice interviewing your teacher. Before you begin, make a list with your group of some questions that you should *not* ask someone when you first meet him or her. Keep adding to this list.

Example: How much do you weigh?
What is your religion?
How much do you make for teaching us?

Are there some questions you could ask in your country that would be unacceptable elsewhere?

After you have discussed what you should not ask, make a list of questions to ask. Try using all verb tenses. When you have finished your list, interview your teacher. Each student should take turns asking a question. Notice that some of the questions listed above are not appropriate for this teacher interview.

4. Interview

What's the story of the mystery student?

5. Read and Discuss

Read the oral history of Yoko Hiyakawa. Discuss the italicized expressions.

6. Act It Out

Practice the following situation with a partner.

Roles: Employer and employee

Situation: A new employee has just received a promotion, even though you have been at the job a year longer. Politely try to show your boss that you are capable of doing that job.

Helpful Phrases

EMPLOYEE	EMPLOYER
I'd like to talk to you about . . .	I'm glad you brought this to my attention.
I really think that . . .	I'll see what can be done.

EMPLOYEE	EMPLOYER
I wanted to know how . . .	Thank you for letting me know.
I appreciate your talking to me.	I'll get back to you soon.

7. Call Up

Make the following phone call. Take notes to report back to the class.

Who? Call a classmate.

Why? You are having a dinner party at your home. Invite your classmates. Give directions to your home.

Helpful Phrases

CALLER	GUEST
Are you free next Friday?	Yes, I think I am. Let me check my calendar.
What time is good for you?	How about a little after six?
Would you like to come for dinner?	Oh, I'd love to! That sounds great. What would you like me to bring?
I'm so glad you can make it.	What's the best way to get to your place?
I'm really looking forward to seeing you.	See you next Friday.

8. Act It Out

Practice the following situation in groups of three.

Roles: Host and two guests

Situation: Two guests who do not know each other arrive at your house for dinner. The first one brings you roses, the second brings a box of candy. The second guest arrives five minutes after the first. You welcome both to your house and make introductions.

Helpful phrases

HOST	GUEST
So good to see you!	It's good to see you, too.
I'm so glad that you could make it.	I'm so happy to be here.
Come on in! Let me take your coat (hat, umbrella)	Thank you.
Oh, these flowers are beautiful! You shouldn't have.	Oh, I'm glad you like them.
Please have a seat. Make yourself at home.	Thanks so much.
What would you like to drink?	Oh, I'd love some _____.
I'd like to introduce you to a good friend of mine. Yoko, this is Sue.	I'm so happy to meet you. I've heard a lot about you.

CHAPTER 4
Jaime Gonzalez

1. Think It Over

Be prepared to express your opinions on these questions in class.

1. What aspects of your job do you dislike? Do you dislike the people you work with, the conditions, the level of stimulation, the salary, the benefits?
2. What would your dream job be? Why? Describe the differences between your dream job and your present job.
3. Have the members of your family become acculturated to life in this country at different rates? Describe how each member of your family has adapted.
4. What advice would you give to family members having problems adjusting to life in a new place?
5. How would you advise a person from your country before he or she moved to another country?

2. One-Minute Speech

Ask two students to give a brief talk in front of the class about any one of the questions above.

3. Conversation Skills

Asking Follow-Up Questions

Often, responses to questions are too brief. It is considered polite to ask follow-up questions to show your interest unless the person seems uncomfortable answering.

1. *Could you tell me more about* your family?
2. *Would you mind telling us more about* what happened?

	3. *Something else I'd like to hear about* is your school.
	4. *I'd like to know* why you decided to come here.
Stronger	5. *I'd love to hear more about* your parents.
Less	6. *What else* can you tell us about your school?
Formal	7. *Tell me about it.*

Practice

With a partner, find out whatever you can about your classmate's mother and/or father. Use follow-up questions in your interview.

Example:
- Student #1: So tell me, what does your father do for a living?
- Student #2: He's retired.
- Student #1: *Could you tell me* what he did before? or *How about* before he was retired?
- Student #2: He was a businessman.
- Student #1: Oh, a businessman. *I'd like to know* what kind of business he was in.
- Student #2: Import–export.
- Student #1: Gee, *I'd love to hear more about* his business.

4. Interview

What's the story of the mystery student?

5. Read and Discuss

Read the oral history of Jaime Gonzalez. Discuss the italicized expressions.

6. Act It Out

Practice the following situation with a partner.

Roles: Superintendent and tenant

Situation: Three months ago, you complained about a leak in your bathroom ceiling. The leak is getting worse and the superintendent has not fixed it. Get him to set a date to repair it.

Helpful Phrases

TENANT	SUPERINTENDENT
Listen, I know you've been very busy, but . . .	I'll take care of it as soon as possible (as soon as I can).
Could you please take care of it right away?	
Can you come this afternoon?	This afternoon is out.
What about tomorrow?	I'll try to take a look at it.
It's an emergency.	Take it easy! Calm down!
I've been waiting for three months now.	There's no reason to get upset.

7. Call Up

Make the following phone call. Take notes to report back to the class.

Who? Call a place in your neighborhood that offers English classes. You can telephone the local library, elementary school, adult education center, or private language school for information.

Why? Your cousin is arriving next month and you need to find an English course for him/her. Ask about the placement exam, the hours and days of the course, the cost, and the number of students in a class. If possible, have the school send you a brochure.

Helpful Phrases

CALLER FOR INFORMATION

I'm calling to find out about . . .
I'd like to know . . .
Could you please tell me . . .
I'd appreciate your sending me a catalogue.
Thanks for your help.

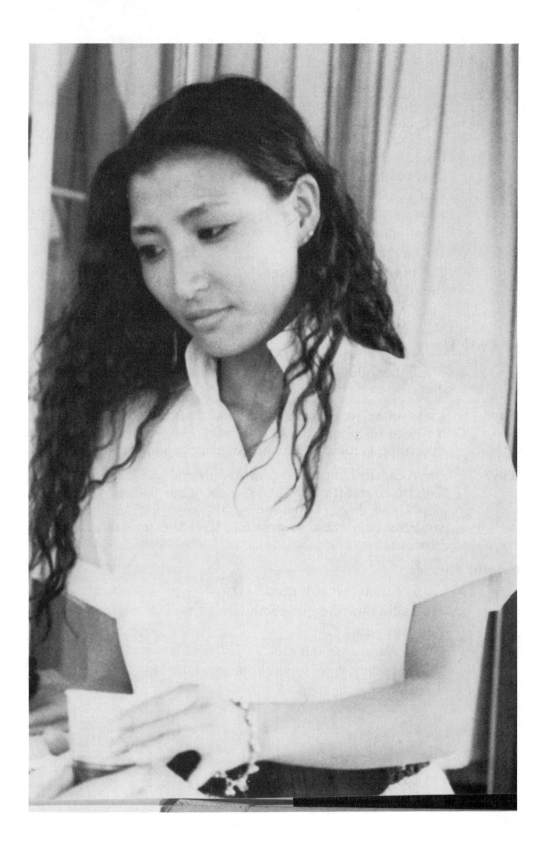

CHAPTER 5
Jeong-Ja Kim

1. Think It Over

Be prepared to express your opinions on these questions in class.

1. What kind of visa do you have? Are you a permanent resident? Are you a citizen? Explain how you got your papers.
2. How do you feel about a person who marries to get permanent resident status?
3. How are unmarried couples living together viewed in your country? Describe how such couples are treated by family and society. Give specific examples. How do you feel about this?
4. Have you ever gambled? Describe your experience.

2. One-Minute Speech

Ask two students to give a brief talk in front of the class about any one of the questions above.

3. Conversation Skills

Hesitating

Sometimes people need time to think before answering a question. But a silent hesitation can be misunderstood as a sign of not understanding the question or of your not wanting to answer. You can show your interest in answering by learning to use these hesitation phrases.

1. Well, . . .
2. Well, you see . . .
3. Well, let me think . . .

4. Let's see now . . .
5. How shall I put it?
6. How can I put it?
7. Mmmmmmmmmmm . . .
8. Ahhhhhhhhh . . .
9. That's a good question.
10. That's an interesting question.
11. In fact, . . .
12. The thing is that . . .
13. I guess that . . .

Practice

With a partner, practice using these hesitation expressions by asking each other difficult questions. You can make up your own questions and/or use the ones below.

Example: Student #1: How long will it take you to learn to speak English fluently?
Student #2: *That's a good question. Well,* I hope in another year.
Question #1: Would you ever consider changing your major (job)?
Question #2: Would you ever consider going to a different school?
Question #3: Why do (don't) you like the American president?
Question #4: Where will you be five (ten) years from now?

4. Interview

What's the story of the mystery student?

5. Read and Discuss

Read the oral history of Jeong-Ja Kim. Discuss the italicized expressions.

6. Act It Out

Practice the following situation with a partner.

Roles: Two co-workers

Situation: One of you has learned that another co-worker you are friendly with is romantically interested in the manager. You know the manager to be a flirt, a drinker, and a gambler. Warn your friend about the manager.

Helpful Phrases

CO-WORKER WHO WARNS	RESPONSE
I don't know how to tell you this, but . . .	That's hard to believe.
I think you ought to know that . . .	Are you kidding? That can't be!
I don't know how to break this to you, but . . .	I appreciate your concern.

7. Call Up

Make the following phone call. Take notes to report back to the class.

Who? Immigration Services, Foreign Student Adviser, Consulate.

Why? What questions do you have about getting a visa or having a visa changed or extended? Plan your questions before calling.

Helpful Phrases

CALLER FOR INFORMATION
I'm calling to find out . . .
I'd like to know . . .
I wonder if you could tell me . . .
Thanks for your help.

CHAPTER 6
Gerard Le Pont

1. Think It Over

Be prepared to express your opinions on these questions in class.

1. How are foreigners viewed in your country? How accurate do you think that view is? Do you have a stereotyped image of foreigners? If so, describe your view.
2. What do your family and neighbors think about your moving to another country? How do they imagine your life is here?
3. Would you marry someone ten years older or younger than you? Would you marry someone of a different race, religion, or nationality? Would you marry someone your parents disapproved of? Explain your answers.

2. One-Minute Speech

Ask two students to give a short talk in front of the class about any one of the questions above.

3. Conversation Skills

Reporting

Another way to hesitate before answering a question is to repeat what a person has asked. This is also a way to make sure you have understood what has been said. Answers are often repeated by the questioner as a way to follow up the original question.

1. *Why did I come? Well . . .*
2. *You asked me why* I came to this country.

3. *You asked me if* I was enjoying my stay here.
4. *You asked me whether* I would go back there again soon.
5. *You wanted to know why* I came here.
6. *You told us that* you came to study.
7. *You said that* you were feeling homesick.

Practice

Practice reporting questions in groups of three.

Example: Student #1: Will you continue studying English next semester?
Student #2: What did he say?
Student #3: Well, *he asked me if I would* continue studying. Yes, I think I will.
Student #1: Are you going to stay in the dormitory?
Student #2: What did she say?
Student #3: *She wanted to know if I was* going to stay in the same place. Well, I hope not!

4. Interview

What's the story of the mystery student?

5. Read and Discuss

Read the oral history of Gerard Le Pont. Discuss the italicized expressions.

6. Act It Out

Practice the following situation with a partner.

Roles: Two good friends

Situation: You haven't seen each other for a long time. When you run into your friend on the street, you want to tell him/her some good news. You may want to report that you are getting married, having a baby, getting a promotion, going to a good school, or living in an inexpensive but beautiful apartment. You are both happy for each other.

Helpful Phrases

OLD FRIEND	RESPONSE
Gee, it's good to see you!	You look wonderful.
It's been a long time.	It sure has.
I have so much to tell you!	What's new?
Guess what!	That's great!
You won't believe this, but . . .	How fantastic!
Wait till you hear this!	Wow, I'm really happy for you!
It's so good to see you again.	That's great news. Congratulations!
Let's get together soon.	Give me a call next week.

7. Call Up

Make the following phone call. Take notes to report back to the class.

Who? A classmate

Why? You have some bad news. Your friend sympathizes and tries to cheer you up. Think of something that has happened to you or to someone you know that you want to tell a classmate. For example, you may know some students who have had their bicycles stolen or their apartments robbed.

Helpful Phrases

CALLER	PERSON CALLED
Have you heard about . . . ?	No, what happened?
I have something terrible to tell you.	Oh, I'm so sorry to hear that.
Something awful has happened.	Oh, I feel terrible for you.
I'm really feeling lousy.	Don't worry! Chin up! You'll get over it.

CHAPTER 7
Dina Rubinov

1. Think It Over

Be prepared to express your opinions on these questions in class.

1. Is it easy to change professions in your country? Explain the opportunities available to a middle-aged person who wants to be retrained or go back to school. Have you ever thought of changing careers? If so, explain. What do you think are some good professions to go into today?
2. Have you ever personally felt any religious persecution? Explain.
3. Is there a religious minority in your country? If so, describe the problems this group has in finding jobs, attending school, living in certain neighborhoods, marrying outside the religion, and gaining any political power. Give examples.
4. Do you think that children should be raised in a religious tradition or be allowed to choose one when they are older? Why?
5. Do you think that children have an easier time learning a language than adults do? Up to what age? Why do you think this is true?

2. One-Minute Speech

Ask two students to give a brief talk in front of the class about any one of the questions above.

3. Conversation Skills

Paraphrasing

Paraphrasing is a good conversational tool for making sure you have understood what is being said. Paraphrasing means restating in your own words what another person has said.

1. *I think what you're saying is that* you feel lonely.
2. *If I understand you correctly,* you are really happy here.
3. *What you want to tell us is that* you were disappointed.
4. *What you mean is that* you'd like to meet some Americans.
5. *What you're trying to say is* that you're homesick.
6. *What you're saying is that* life here is overwhelming.
7. *In other words,* you like what you see.

Less Formal
8. *You mean* you want to change your major.

Rephrasing

When the person you are talking to misunderstands you, it is better to rephrase what you have said instead of repeating the same thing. These expressions can help you to introduce your restatement.

1. *I'd like to say that* I was surprised when I found out.
2. *What I want to say is* that you have missed my point.
3. *What I was trying to tell you was* how important it is to learn English.
4. *What I really meant was that* it could have been done.
5. *I really want to say that* you should have come.
6. *I'm trying to tell you that* it's unfair.

Less Formal
7. *I mean that* you could have done it.
8. *Actually,* I was upset.

Practice

Choose a partner and ask each other the following questions. Add your own questions, too. After listening to your partner's response, paraphrase his/her answer.

Example: Student #1: Why did you come to the United States?
               Student #2: Let's see now . . . how shall I put it? I guess that I wasn't very excited about the political science department in my country. So I felt that it would help me much more to study here.

	Student #1:	*In other words,* you feel that studying political science here will help your professional opportunities at home.
	Student #2:	Yes, that's what I mean.

If Student #1 has misunderstood you, try to rephrase what you said.

Example:	Student #2:	No, it's not that. *What I want to say is that* the political science department is more challenging here.
	Student #1:	Oh, I see.

4. Interview

What's the story of the mystery student?

5. Read and Discuss

Read the oral history of Dina Rubinov. Discuss the italicized expressions.

6. Act It Out

Practice the following situations with a partner.

Roles: Teacher and student

Situation:

1. You are going to miss class next Monday. Explain why. Find out what you will miss.
2. It's the end of the semester. You have enjoyed the class very much. Tell the teacher.

Helpful Phrases

STUDENT	TEACHER
Could I speak to you for a moment?	
I'm awfully sorry, but I won't be able to make it to class next Monday.	Oh, I'm sorry you won't be here.
Would you mind keeping any handouts for me?	Not at all.

STUDENT	TEACHER
How can I make up the class?	
I'd like to know the assignment for next week.	
I really enjoyed being in this class.	I'm so glad to hear that.
I appreciate all your help.	I've enjoyed having you in class, too.
I've learned so much.	
I've really gotten a lot out of it.	
This is one of the best courses I've ever taken.	

7. Call Up

Make the following phone call. Take notes to report back to the class.

Who? Look through the local newspaper for an advertised job related to your field.

Why? Ask for a fuller description of the job. Ask what the job entails, how much experience is needed, what the benefits are, what the salary range is, and what other qualifications are needed.

Helpful Phrases

JOB SEEKER

I'm interested in the position of . . . that you advertised in this Sunday's . . .

Could you tell me . . . ?

I'd like to know . . .

CHAPTER 8
Hector Rodriguez

1. Think It Over

Be prepared to express your opinions on these questions in class.

1. There are over one million illegal aliens living in the United States. Since they are living in this country, should the United States educate them and help them financially? Should more illegal aliens be prevented from coming in? If so, what measures would you recommend?
2. A United States federal law states that illegal aliens who have lived in the United States continuously since January 1, 1982, can apply for temporary residence and eventually citizenship. Those who entered after January 1982, are subject to deportation, and employers who hire them can be penalized. How do you feel about this law?
3. Does your country have a problem with illegal aliens? Describe the situation and how your country deals with it.
4. How would you feel if your spouse earned more money than you? Explain.
5. How do you feel about a woman with children working outside the home? Explain.

2. One-Minute Speech

Ask two students to give a brief talk in front of the class about any one of the questions above.

3. Conversation Skills
Listening Attentively

If you watch an American listen while someone else is speaking, you will notice that the American nods and says short phrases to assure the speaker that he or she is listening attentively. Standing there motionless and saying nothing can be interpreted as signs of disinterest, lack of understanding, and even anger. Learn to use these listening words in every conversation.

AGREEMENT	15. Terrific!	28. Oh?
1. Mmm-hmm.	16. Wonderful!	29. Oh, really?
2. Uh-huh.	17. Fantastic!	DISAGREEMENT
3. Yes.	SURPRISE	30. Oh, no.
4. Yeah.	18. Gee!	31. Uh-uh.
5. Right.	19. Oh, really?	32. Euh!
6. Sure.	20. What?	33. Impossible!
7. I see.	21. Huh?	34. Ridiculous!
8. I know.	22. My goodness!	35. Oh, come on!
9. Exactly.	23. No kidding!	36. No way!
10. I agree.	24. Wow!	CONTINUE
11. Of course.	DOUBT	37. And then?
12. Definitely.	25. Maybe.	38. Go on!
DELIGHT	26. Well . . .	39. Well?
13. Interesting!	27. Hmm.	40. What else?
14. Great!		

Practice

With a partner, take turns telling each other stories about times when you were afraid. While your partner is the storyteller, you should be constantly giving him/her the sense that you are listening attentively. Use the words above to show your interest.

Example: Student #1: I'd like to tell you about a time when I was hiking on a glacier in Switzerland.
Student #2: *Wow! Go on!*
Student #1: During the hike, the weather changed and I couldn't see one foot in front of me because of the fog.
Student #2: *My goodness! And then?*

4. Interview

What's the story of the mystery student?

5. Read and Discuss

Read the oral history of Hector Rodriguez. Discuss the italicized expressions.

6. Act It Out

Practice the following situation in pairs.

Roles: Two good friends

Situation: Is there something that you are upset about (for example, class, job, family, money)? Tell your friend about it, and he or she will try to comfort you.

Helpful Phrases

UPSET FRIEND	COMFORTING FRIEND
I'm furious (outraged, disgusted, mad).	I understand how you must feel.
It's so unfair (infuriating).	You're (absolutely) right.
It really makes me angry (burns me up).	It would make me angry, too.
I feel so upset with . . .	I don't blame you.
I feel like quitting (changing schools).	
I feel like telling him/her what I think.	
How could that have happened?	I really don't understand it, either.
I just can't believe it!	Neither can I!
After all my hard work!	You're so right.
I really can't stand . . .	Don't let it get to you.
I can't take it.	Forget about it.
It's really getting to me.	Come on! Pull yourself together!

7. Call Up

Make the following phone call. Take notes to report back to the class.

Who? Friend or boss

Why? You are going to be late. Excuse yourself and give a reason.

Helpful Phrases

CALLER	PERSON CALLED
I'm awfully sorry, but I won't be able to be there on time.	Come as soon as you can.
I won't be able to make it on time.	Don't worry about it.
I got caught up at work (school).	See you later then.
I got stuck in traffic.	Oh, that's too bad.
My car broke down.	Oh, well.
I overslept. My alarm clock didn't ring.	Oh, no!
The subway was delayed.	Oh, really?
I lost track of the time.	

CHAPTER 9
May Chang

1. Think It Over

Be prepared to express your opinions on these questions in class.

1. Do unmarried women leave their families and live on their own in your country? What are the consequences of doing so? How does the society view it? Explain.
2. Do you think that the family unit in your country is more closely knit than in other countries? Describe the main differences you see in relationships among siblings, and among children and their parents and grandparents.
3. Are dating practices in this country very different from those in your country? Explain.
4. How have you changed as a result of living in another culture (for example, your name, eating habits, dress, thinking style)? What do you *not* want to change?

2. One-Minute Speech

Ask two students to give a brief talk in front of the class about any one of the questions above.

3. Conversation Skills
Asking for Repetition

When you don't understand something, ask the person to repeat what he or she has said. It is much better to do that than to pretend you have understood. Here are various ways to ask for repetition.

1. Would you mind repeating that?
2. Excuse me, what was that you said?
3. Pardon, what did you say?
4. Could you please repeat that?
5. I didn't quite follow what you said.
6. Sorry, what was that?

Informal
7. What?
8. What was that?
9. I didn't get that.
10. I didn't catch what you said.

Practice

With a partner, take turns telling each other about your family trees. Describe all your family relationships (for example, any sisters, brothers, stepparents, stepchildren, in-laws, great-grandparents, second cousins, half-brothers). If you have trouble following your partner's description, ask him/her to repeat.

Example: Student #1: I have one half-sister, who is the daughter of my father before he married my mother.
Student #2: *Could you please repeat that? I didn't quite follow what you said.*

4. Interview

What's the story of the mystery student?

5. Read and Discuss

Read the oral history of May Chang. Discuss the italicized expressions.

6. Act It Out

Practice the following situation in pairs.

Roles: Two friends

Situation: Try to convince your friend to change his/her mind about something. After much persuasion, your friend gives in. You may want to persuade your friend to go with you to an aerobics class, to a Weight Watchers meeting, to an Indian restaurant, or to the park to jog.

Helpful Phrases

PERSUASIVE FRIEND	RESPONSE
Come on!	I'm much too busy to . . .
Just try it!	I have a lot of things to do.
You won't regret it.	I don't feel like it.
Why not?	I don't feel like going.
If you come, you'll . . .	I'm not in the mood.
	I'm not up to it.

Changing Your Mind

Well, if you insist . . .
Now that I think about it . . .
On second thought . . .

7. Call Up

Make the following phone call. Take notes to report back to the class.

Who? A classmate

Why? You are calling to turn down an invitation. Be apologetic. Give a reason.

Helpful Phrases

CALLER	PERSON CALLED
I'm awfully sorry, but I won't be able to make it tonight.	That's a pity!
I didn't realize it before, but . . .	That's really too bad!
I hope it isn't too much of an inconvenience.	That's okay. Not at all.

CALLER	PERSON CALLED
I feel terrible, but . . .	Don't worry. We'll do it another time.
It's really a shame I can't make it.	I was looking forward to seeing you.
How about some time next week?	Give me a call when you're free.

CHAPTER 10
Taeb Omar

1. Think It Over

Be prepared to express your own opinions on these questions in class.

1. Do you think that people have more opportunities in other countries than in your country? Give examples.
2. Is there a draft system in your country? If so, explain how it works. How do you feel about it?
3. Is there any war in which you would have been a draft dodger? Give your reasons. Do you feel that draft dodgers should be punished? Why or why not?

2. One-Minute Speech

Ask two students to give a brief talk in front of the class about any one of the questions above.

3. Conversation Skills

Interrupting

Interrupting, when done politely, can be a useful conversational tool. Learn how to interrupt with these expressions.

1. Oh, excuse me, but . . .
2. May I say something?
3. May I interrupt you for a minute?
4. I'd like to add something.
5. I'd just like to say that . . .
6. Sorry to interrupt you, but . . .

Informal 7. Oh, I just thought of something.
8. That reminds me . . .
9. By the way, . . .
10. Before I forget, . . .

Practice

With two of your classmates, share your experiences of being a student. Was it easy to get information (for example, about courses)? Were the staff people (for example, secretaries, receptionists, counselors, teachers) helpful? Try to interrupt your classmates politely whenever you want to ask or say something.

Example: Student #1: When I called up for information, I was put on hold for ten minutes. I was so angry that . . .
Student #2: *Before I forget,* I want to tell you about what happened when I called. The receptionist disconnected me. So when . . .
Student #3: *That reminds me* of what happened to me today . . .

4. Interview

What's the story of the mystery student?

5. Read and Discuss

Read the oral history of Taeb Omar. Discuss the italicized expressions.

6. Act It Out

Practice the following situation in pairs.

Roles: Host and guest

Situation: One of you has been invited to the other's home for a delicious meal. The host keeps trying to get the guest to eat more. The guest politely refuses the food.

Helpful Phrases

HOST	GUEST
Please, take some more!	Everything is delicious, but I'm really quite full.
Have another piece!	I think I've had enough, thank you.
You've hardly eaten anything.	Gosh, I'm so stuffed. I really couldn't eat another bite.
You've hardly touched your food.	I'm leaving room for dessert.
Didn't you like it?	I don't have much of an appetite.
	I'm on a diet.

7. Call Up

Make the following phone call. Take notes to report back to the class.

Who? A classmate

Why? Find out about a good restaurant in town. Get the name and address. Ask your friend to recommend something to order.

Helpful Phrases

PERSON RECOMMENDING

Be sure to try . . .
Don't forget to order . . .
Save room for dessert.
Skip the coffee (the appetizers, the salad).

CHAPTER 11
Heidi Tobler

1. Think It Over

Be prepared to express your opinions on these questions in class.

1. Is your profession different from your parents' professions? How did you choose your career? How did your family feel about your career choice? What influence did they have on your choice?
2. Do you feel that privacy is valued more in other cultures than in your own? Do you feel there is a lack of concern for others in those cultures? Is your privacy intruded upon in your country? If so, how?

2. One-Minute Speech

Ask two students to give a brief talk in front of the class about any one of the questions above.

3. Conversation Skills

Returning to the Story

Sometimes people get sidetracked when talking. Here are some useful expressions to lead you back to your story.

1. Well, . . .
2. Anyway, . . .
3. As I was saying, . . .
4. To get back to what I was saying, . . .
5. To return to the subject, . . .

6. To return to what I was saying,
7. Going back to what I said earlier,
8. Where was I?

Practice

Come to class prepared to tell a partner about an interesting news article you read. Be specific; include where, when, what, why, and how. Also, tell why you chose this story. Your neighbor will interrupt you while you are talking. Use the above expressions to get back to your story.

Example: Student #1: I just read an article in *The New York Times* about the increase in school dropouts.
Student #2: Oh, when did you see that article?
Student #1: Yesterday. *Anyway, as I was saying,* the dropout rate is a terrible problem.

4. Interview

What's the story of the mystery student?

5. Read and Discuss

Read the oral history of Heidi Tobler. Discuss the italicized expressions.

6. Act It Out

Practice the following situation in pairs.

Roles: Two neighbors

Situation: You meet in the hallway or at a corner laundromat. Make small talk—that is, discuss the weather, family, and work.

Helpful Phrases

FRIENDLY NEIGHBOR

How are you doing? What have you been up to?
I haven't seen you around for a while.
The weather's been crazy (awful, great) lately.
Are you getting tired of this heat (rain, snow, cold)?
Working as hard as usual?

FRIENDLY NEIGHBOR

How's the family doing?
How's your roommate doing?
How's everybody doing?
Have a good day! Good to see you.
My best to your sister (roommate).
Give my regards to your wife (husband).

7. Call Up

Make the following phone call. Take notes to report back to the class.

Who? A classmate

Why? An impolite classmate asks you intrusive questions about your life. Don't answer them. Try to discourage your classmate from asking any more questions.

Helpful Phrases

NOSY PERSON	RESPONSE
You look sad today. What's bothering you?	I'm sorry but I don't have time to talk now.
Tell me what's going on.	I'm late for class (work).
I heard you arguing with . . .	I'm afraid I've got to hang up now.
What's the story?	Sorry, to rush off like this but I'm awfully late.
	I'd rather not say.
	I'd really appreciate your not asking me that.

CHAPTER 12
Ali Fahrid

1. Think It Over

Be prepared to express your opinions on these questions in class.

1. Was the education and/or job experience you received in your country accepted outside of your country? Describe your experience.
2. If you felt that your boss was wrong, how would you handle the situation?
   a. do what he said, in spite of your better judgment
   b. do what he said and try to prove he was wrong indirectly
   c. tell him you thought he was wrong, but do as he said
   d. tell him that he was wrong and refuse to follow his orders
   e. say nothing to him and do what you think is right

   Explain your choice. Has this ever happened to you?
3. What can you tell about a person from the way he or she dresses? Do the guidelines followed in your country work elsewhere?

2. One-Minute Speech

Ask two students to give a brief talk in front of the class about any one of the questions above.

3. Conversation Skills

Asking for Response

When giving an opinion, many people like to get responses from those who are listening. Try using these phrases to elicit others' responses.

1. What do you think?
2. How do you feel about that?
3. Don't you agree?
4. Isn't that so?
5. Isn't that true?
6. Do you know what I mean?

Practice:

In a group of four, state your feelings about the following quotations. Use the expressions above to get others to express their opinions.

Quotation #1: Religion is what keeps the poor from murdering the rich. *(Napoleon)*

Quotation #2: Women's emancipation has in various ways made marriage more difficult. *(Bertrand Russell)*

4. Interview

What's the story of the mystery student?

5. Read and Discuss

Read the oral history of Ali Fahrid. Discuss the italicized expressions.

6. Act It Out

Practice the following situation with a partner.

Roles: Two friends

Situation: You want to apologize to a friend for a mistake that you made. Make up a situation or follow these suggestions:

1. You gave your friend a check that bounced.
2. You forgot a lunch date that you had with your friend.

Helpful Phrases

APOLOGIZER	RESPONSE
How could I have done that?	Don't worry about it! Relax!
I'm terribly (awfully, really) sorry.	It could have happened to anyone.
I don't know how I could have made such a terrible mistake.	I should have warned (told) you.
I don't know how it slipped my mind.	I should have reminded you.
I don't know how I could have done that.	It's my fault.
Please excuse me.	It's nothing to get upset about.
I hope you'll forgive me.	Of course I will.

7. Call Up

Make the following phone call. Take notes to report back to the class.

Who? A hotel or motel

Why? Your uncle is coming to visit for a week and your home is too small a place for him to stay. Find out the price and services of two hotels or motels nearby. Get descriptions of the rooms, the exact address of each place, and directions.

Helpful Phrases

CALLER
I'm calling to find out . . .
Thank you for the information.
I'll get back to you later.

CHAPTER 13
Alejandra Maldonado

1. Think It Over

Be prepared to express your opinions on these questions in class.

1. What stereotypes do people from other countries have of people from your country? How accurate are they?
2. Did you have problems finding a place to live here? Describe how you went about apartment-hunting. Compare what you did here to what you would do in your country to find a place to live.
3. Do people keep pets in your country? Which pets? How are they treated? Compare the way you have seen dogs treated in other countries with the way they are treated in your country.

2. One-Minute Speech

Ask two students to give a brief talk in front of the class about any one of the questions above.

3. Conversation Skills

Reacting Positively

When you agree with or approve of something you've heard, there are different levels of reactions you can use, some more formal than others. Try these expressions.

1. I agree.
2. That sounds good.
3. Good for you!
4. That's wonderful (great, terrific, fantastic, amazing).
5. Please go on.

Informal
6. Go on! Tell me more!
7. Gosh, how fantastic!
8. Isn't that something?
9. Wow, that's incredible!
10. Gee, that's great!
11. Well, you are really something!
12. Absolutely, that's it.

Reacting Negatively

Being able to show how strongly you disagree is important. Do you feel the different levels of anger implied in these phrases? Which expressions would you use with your teacher or your boss?

1. That may be true, but . . .
2. I understand what you're saying, but . . .
3. The problem with that is . . .
4. Well, I don't really agree.
5. I'm afraid I disagree.

Very Strong
6. How could you have?
7. What made you do that?
8. Why did you do that?
9. Oh no, that can't be!
10. You shouldn't have . . .
11. I wish you hadn't . . .
12. I don't understand why . . .

Practice

Practice making negative and positive reactions to a statement. With a partner, use the statements below or make up your own.

1. I'm going to get married (divorced, promoted, fired, laid off).
2. I received a scholarship (a raise, my green card).
3. I lost my wallet (my keys, my address book).
4. I failed the midterm (the driver's test).

4. Interview

What's the story of the mystery student?

5. Read and Discuss

Read the oral history of Alejandra Maldonado. Discuss the italicized expressions.

6. Act It Out

Practice the following situation in pairs.

Roles: Two strangers

Situation: You are both seated in a restaurant. Seated next to one of you is a big dog, which is licking your neighbor's leg. The dog owner is also smoking a cigar. Try to get the dog owner to control his dog and to put out his cigar.

Helpful Phrases

PERSON WHO IS BOTHERED	RESPONSE
Excuse me, but would it be possible for you to . . . ?	I'm terribly sorry.
I'd really appreciate it if you would . . .	He's a gentle dog.
Would you mind putting out your cigar?	I'm almost through.
Do you think you could . . . ?	Is it really bothering (annoying) you?
Excuse me, but your . . . is really bothering me.	

7. Call Up

Make the following phone call. Take notes to report back to class.

Who? A real estate agent

Why? Cut out an advertisement for a house or an apartment from the real estate section of your local newspaper. Call and find out more information about the place. Ask about the location, the size, the price, the security deposit, the condition, the neighborhood, and the appliances.

Helpful Phrases

CALLER

Could you please tell me if the apartment on 16th Street is still available?
I'd like to know if . . . ?
Could you tell me a little bit about the neighborhood?
What's the building (house) like?
What floor is it on?
Which direction does it face?
Is the area safe?
How close is public transportation?

CHAPTER 14
Stanley Wolinski

1. Think It Over

Be prepared to express your opinions on these questions in class.

1. What have you found to be the most difficult thing about learning English? What has helped you the most in learning English? What is the most frustrating part about learning a language?
2. Did your status change when you moved to another city or country? Describe the change and how you reacted to it.
3. Why did you move to another city or country? Did you get what you came for?
4. What did you like or dislike about the educational system in your country? Give specific examples.

2. One-Minute Speech

Ask two students to give a brief talk in front of the class about any one of the questions above.

3. Conversation Skills

Giving Suggestions

By giving suggestions, you show your active interest in the other person. Notice the different levels of formality in the expressions below.

Polite	1. Wouldn't it be better if . . .
	2. Wouldn't it be a good idea to . . .
Formal	3. What I advise you to do is . . .
	4. I suggest that you . . .
	5. I recommend doing that.
	6. Perhaps you could . . .
Less Formal	7. You can always . . .
	8. Why don't you . . .
	9. How about . . .
	10. Why not . . .
	11. If I were you, I'd . . .
Informal	12. If I were in your shoes, I'd . . .
Strong	13. You'd better . . .

Accepting Suggestions

There are different degrees of accepting a suggestion that you like. Some expressions show more enthusiasm than others. Can you feel the differences among the expressions listed below?

Hesitant	1. Perhaps that would work.
	2. Maybe I should try that.
	3. Maybe I'll give that a try.
	4. That sounds like it might work out.
Stronger	5. I think you've got something there.
	6. Hmm . . . that sounds like a good idea.
	7. Oh, that's tempting!
	8. Yes, why don't I?
Informal	9. What do you know! Maybe you have something there.

Turning Down Suggestions

When turning down a suggestion, you can respond in three ways: ask for another suggestion, soften your rejection, or say a strong no.

1. Is there anything else you can suggest?
2. Do you have any other ideas?
3. Is there anything else you would do in my position?
4. That's not quite what I want.
5. No, that's not exactly what I had in mind.
6. I'm not sure that would work.
7. I think you've misunderstood me.
8. That doesn't sound too good. (interesting, hopeful)

Stronger 9. That's not what I need.
10. I don't see any advantage in doing that.
11. No, that's no good.
12. That wouldn't work.

Practice

With a partner, take turns giving suggestions and responding to the suggestions. One of you will state a problem, and then the other will give advice. Use the problems below or make up your own.

1. My teacher doesn't like me.
2. I'm running out of money for this month.
3. The cockroaches are taking over my apartment.
4. People in this country speak too quickly.
5. I'm finding it difficult to meet people.
6. I miss my parents.

4. Interview

What's the story of the mystery student?

5. Read and Discuss

Read the oral history of Stanley Wolinski. Discuss the italicized expressions.

6. Act It Out

Practice the following situation with a partner.

Roles: Teacher and student

Situation: Try teaching a classmate some expressions from your region (for example, hello, good-bye, how are you, thank you, you're welcome, I love you). Make sure you instruct your classmate of the correct pronunciation.

Helpful Phrases

TEACHER

Yes, you've almost got it.
Pretty good.
Try it again.
Repeat after me.
It sounds like . . .
Put your tongue . . .
Round your lips.
Now you sound like a native.

7. Call Up

Make the following phone call. Take notes to report back to the class.

Who? Your classmate.

Why? You need advice on where to go in town or on a trip you are planning to take to your classmate's country. Give each other advice on where to go, what to eat, where to stay, and what to buy. Also, advise your classmate where not to go.

Helpful Phrases

NEWCOMER	ADVISER
Do you know where there is a good place to . . . ?	I suggest going (not going) . . .
What I would love to see is . . .	I recommend that you take (not take) . . .
What's the best way to get there?	I advise you to go (not to go) . . .
	How much do you plan on spending?
	What would you like to do?
	If I were you, I'd . . .
	Whatever you do, don't miss . . .

CHAPTER 15
Marie Lionne

1. Think It Over

Be prepared to express your opinions on these questions in class.

1. What qualities are important in choosing a spouse? Rate the following in order of importance. Add any qualities not listed.

family background	generosity	profession
financial security	intelligence	virginity
height	educational background	creativity
weight	submissiveness	spontaneity
attractiveness	aggressiveness	race
age	political ideas	religion
open-mindedness	sense of humor	neatness
even-tempered	dependability	faithfulness

2. Is there a "brain drain" in your country? Do you think that people owe it to their countries to return even though they may be better off financially in another country?

2. One-Minute Speech

Ask two students to give a brief talk in front of the class about any one of the questions above.

3. Conversation Skills

Ending a Conversation

Most Americans expect to hear an explanation when a conversation is being ended. Ending abruptly may make you seem rude or angry. Use these expressions to sound polite. Try to give a reason for leaving.

1. I'm awfully sorry, but I have to run. I have to catch the five o'clock train.
2. I'm afraid that I have to go now. Someone is waiting for me downstairs.
3. Gee, I have an appointment at three o'clock. I have to rush off now.
4. Oh, it's getting late. I'd better be going.
5. Well, I think that's about it. I'd better be going. My schedule is really tight.

Less Formal
6. Oops! My goodness! Look at the time! I should be going.

Practice

With a partner, try out the above expressions in these situations:

1. with a classmate you met on the street
2. with a business associate after a meeting
3. with the host of a party you attended
4. with an old friend you haven't seen in years

4. Interview

What's the story of the mystery student?

5. Read and Discuss

Read the oral history of Marie Lionne. Discuss the italicized expressions.

6. Act It Out

Practice the following situation with a partner.

Roles: Two friends

Situation: Your friend's boyfriend/girlfriend has just left. To cheer your friend up, you compliment his/her appearance.

Helpful Phrases

COMPLIMENT GIVER	RECEIVER OF COMPLIMENTS
I really like your haircut.	Do you really like it? I'm still trying to get used to it.
What a beautiful watch you have!	Oh, I've had it for years. I'm glad you like it.
You've really been losing weight.	Do you really think so?
You look like you're in great shape.	Thanks.
How well you speak English!	Not as well as you!

7. Call Up

Make the following phone call. Take notes to report back to the class.

Who? A classmate

Why? Your friend is returning to his country. Say good-bye.

Helpful Phrases

YOU	RESPONSE
I can't believe you're really leaving!	I can't believe it, either.
Don't forget to write.	Don't worry, I won't.
Don't forget to call me when you get back.	
I wish I were going with you.	I wish you could come, too.

YOU	RESPONSE
Can you fit me inside your suitcase?	I'll miss you.
When will you be back?	
Gosh, I envy you.	
Have a wonderful trip!	

CHAPTER 16
Koji Watanabe

1. Think It Over

Be prepared to express your opinions on these questions in class.

1. Have you ever lived alone? How did you or do you like it? Explain.
2. How different is the style of eating in your culture from that of other cultures? How do you feel about people eating between meals, on buses, on the job, and while walking down the street? Have you gained or lost weight when you went to another country? Explain.
3. If there were a sign that said "No eating or smoking in this classroom," would you obey it? Would people in your country obey a sign like that?
4. Have you ever had anything stolen? Describe the incident.

2. One-Minute Speech

Ask two students to give a brief talk in front of the class about any one of the questions above.

3. Conversation Skills

Thanking

A simple "thank you" is often not enough. Which of the following expressions of gratitude could you use for a teacher whose class you enjoyed, a friend who has listened to your problems, and a business associate who has helped you?

1. I've really gotten a lot out of this.
2. I really appreciate your concern (help).
3. Thanks for your time (advice, help, ideas).
4. You've really made me think.
5. Thanks a million (a lot, so much).
6. It's been good (wonderful, great, terrific) talking with you.
7. How can I ever thank you enough?
8. How can I thank you enough for all you've done for me?
9. You've really been a (great) help.
10. What a help this has been!
11. What a relief to get all this off my chest!
12. Thanks for putting up with me.
13. I hope I haven't taken up too much of your time.

Responding to Thanks

A person who is thanked often gives thanks in response. Practice these different ways of saying "You're welcome" in English.

1. It's been a pleasure talking to you.
2. It's really been good talking to you.
3. I've enjoyed talking to you.
4. I'm glad that you found this helpful.
5. I'm happy to be of help.
6. My pleasure.
7. You're very welcome.
8. No trouble at all.
   Often a person offers more help when thanked.
9. Let me know if I can be of any more help.
10. Let me know how things work out.
11. Keep in touch.

Practice

With a partner, try using these expressions of thanking and responding to thanks in these situations. Think of other situations in which you need to thank someone.

1. a friend who treated you to dinner
2. a business associate who took you out to lunch
3. a teacher who spent extra time with you to explain an assignment
4. a salesperson who made an effort to find a pair of shoes for you

4. Interview

What's the story of the mystery student?

5. Read and Discuss

Read the oral history of Koji Watanabe. Discuss the italicized expressions.

6. Act It Out

Practice the following situation with a partner.

Roles: You and co-worker

Situation: You forgot to put money in your wallet before going to work. You need to borrow ten dollars to pay for the meal you have just eaten.

Helpful Phrases

BORROWER	LENDER
I don't know how I could have done that.	Don't worry. I can lend you some money.
I feel so silly.	Oh, it doesn't matter. Take this money.
Oh no, I couldn't let you pay.	Yes. You can pay me back later.
Are you sure you have enough?	More than enough.

CHAPTER 16

BORROWER	LENDER
Oh, I feel terrible.	My pleasure.
I'll pay you back on _____.	Don't worry about it.
Thanks a million.	You're very welcome.

7. Call Up

Make the following phone call. Take notes to report back to the class.

Who? A classmate

Why? Someone in the class took your wallet from your briefcase. You think you saw the person who did it. Describe the person (someone from your class) and see if your partner can guess who it was from your description.

Helpful Phrases

DESCRIBER	GUESSER
The person was about _____ feet tall.	Could it have been _____?
He/she was sort of on the heavy side.	Perhaps it was _____.
His/her hair was around shoulder length.	Maybe it was _____.
It was kind of curly (straight, wavy, long)	Was it _____?
I think that he/she is in his/her early (late, mid-) twenties.	It must have been _____.
The person had a turned-up (stubby, flat, hooked) nose.	
I believe he/she was wearing a tan sweater.	
He was partly bald.	
He had a receding hairline and long sideburns.	
He/she had freckles (a mole, a beauty mark).	

CHAPTER 17
Kenny Lee

1. Think It Over

Be prepared to express your opinions on these questions in class.

1. How has living abroad changed your view of your own country? Have you returned to your country since you left? If so, describe how you reacted upon your return.
2. Do you fear having "culture shock" when you return to your country? If so, explain why.
3. Do you have problems understanding a foreigner's sense of humor? Explain.

2. One-Minute Speech

Ask two students to give a brief talk in front of the class about any one of the questions above.

3. Conversation Skills

Leaving

Here are some ways Americans end their conversations without saying good-bye. To show interest in another person, Americans often talk about getting together again, sometimes without really meaning it. Which of the following expressions suggest that a definite date is expected?

1. See you.
2. See you soon.
3. Let's get together again soon.

4. Do call.
5. Give me a call.
6. How about dinner next week?
7. Let me know when you're free.
8. How about getting together for lunch?
9. How about having a drink next week?
10. Let me know how you're doing.
11. Maybe we can get together again soon.
12. If you're ever in the neighborhood, drop by.
13. Take care.
14. Take it easy.

Responses

1. Sounds great!
2. Terrific!
3. Okay. I'll let you know when I'm free.
4. See you later.
5. I'll call you next week.
6. Sure, sounds good.

Practice

Combine the expressions you have learned for ending a conversation with the expressions for leaving listed above. Practice these situations with a partner.

1. a classmate you ran into on the street
2. a business associate after a meeting
3. the host of a party you attended
4. an old friend you haven't seen in years

4. Interview

What's the story of the mystery student?

5. Read and Discuss

Read the oral history of Kenny Lee. Discuss the italicized expressions.

6. Act It Out

Practice the following situation in front of the class.

Go to a bookstore or library and get a joke book. Find a joke that you like and understand. If you cannot find a joke that you like, try telling the class a joke from your country. Be prepared to explain to your classmates why the joke is funny. Make sure you pick a joke that will not offend anybody.

Expressions for Listener

Would you mind slowing down?
Would you please repeat the last part?
I'm afraid I didn't understand it. What was the point?
I don't really get it. Would you mind explaining it?

7. Call Up

Make the following phone call. Take notes to report back to the class.

Who? Two different airlines or a travel agent

Why? Where would you like to travel? Find out the fastest and cheapest ways to get there. Usually there are many conditions for a cheap flight. Find out if the fare is refundable if you cancel or miss the flight.

Helpful Phrases

CALLER

I'd like to find out about your flights to . . .
Could you tell me if there are any seats left?
What are the restrictions?
When do I have to purchase my ticket by?
Can I leave the return flight open?
Is it cheaper to fly during the week?
If I have to cancel my ticket, will I get a full refund?

CHAPTER 18
José Ojeda

1. Think It Over

Be prepared to express your opinions on these questions in class.

1. What have been your experiences as a traveler? Describe a trip you took (or plan to take) to another country. Compare that country to your country.
2. How efficient are the public services (for example, mail, phone, transportation) in your country? Explain.
3. Is it easy to travel around your country freely? Describe the situation.
4. How is your country's currency doing against the dollar? Explain how this has affected your life style.
5. Compare the differences in cost of living in two countries that you know. Include rent, food, gasoline, clothing, books, records, and public transportation in your answer.

2. One-Minute Speech

Ask two students to give a brief talk in front of the class about any one of the questions above.

3. Interview

What's the story of the mystery student?

4. Read and Discuss

Read the oral history of José Ojeda. Discuss the italicized expressions.

5. Act It Out

Practice the following situation with a partner.

1. Roles: Classmates

Situation: It is the end of the semester. You are returning to your home countries. Say good-bye to everyone. Go around the room. Find out your classmates' plans.

Helpful Phrases

SAYING GOOD-BYE

I really enjoyed meeting you.
It was a pleasure to be in class with you this semester.
I hope to be able to visit (see, talk to) you soon.
I'll call (write, keep in touch, keep you posted).
Don't forget to call (write, keep in touch, keep me posted).
Gee, I wish I didn't have to go.
I wish you were coming with me.
Take down my address. It's . . .
It's really been wonderful being here.
I'll be back before you know it.
Why don't you come visit me?
I'm really going to miss . . .

ASKING ABOUT PLANS	RESPONSE
So, what do you plan on doing next semester?	What I'd like to do is . . .
Where are you off to?	Where I'd like to go is . . .
What do you have in mind?	I hope to . . .
	I plan to . . .

2. Roles: Two classmates

Situation: School has been over for two months. You bump into an old classmate on the street. You haven't seen or heard from him/her since the end of the semester. Greet each other.

Helpful Phrases

CLASSMATE	RESPONSE
Gee, it's been ages!	Yes, it's been a long time.
You really look terrific.	So do you.
You haven't changed a bit.	Neither have you.

CLASSMATE	RESPONSE
Oh, it's so good to see you again.	I'm happy to see you, too.
I'm delighted to see you again.	
What a coincidence to run into you!	Yes, how about that!
I've been meaning to call (visit) you.	So have I.
I was just thinking about you the other day.	So was I.
I can't wait to hear all your news.	I can't wait to tell you everything.

6. Call Up

Make the following phone call. Take notes to report back to the class.

Who? A classmate

Why? You need help. Politely ask a classmate to help you. Think of a situation or use the following examples: ask for a lift to your apartment, for help in moving, or help you with your homework.

Helpful Phrases

CALLER	RESPONSE	NEGATIVE RESPONSE
I wonder if you have any free time on. . .	Sure. What can I do for you?	I'm sorry, but I have other plans.
Would it be at all possible for you to . . .	I'd love to.	I'd love to help, but . . .
If it's not too much trouble, I wanted to know if you could . . .	It's no trouble at all.	That would be great, but . . .
If you don't mind, I would really appreciate your help.	My pleasure.	I wish I had time.

CALLER	RESPONSE	NEGATIVE RESPONSE
I really appreciate it.	I'm glad I can help.	I'm much too busy right now.
That's really nice of you.	Sure, anytime.	My schedule is packed.
		Another time perhaps.

APPENDIX ONE
Vocabulary of Feelings

1. Happy
2. Caring
3. Depressed
4. Inadequate
5. Confused
6. Hurt
7. Angry
8. Lonely

1. Happy
   I feel pleased
     satisfied
     cheerful
     delighted
     wonderful
     great
   I feel alive
     in great spirits
     ecstatic
     overjoyed
     thrilled
   I'm on cloud nine

2. Caring
   I appreciate
   I'm fond of
   I feel concern for
   I'm touched by
   I'm taken with
     infatuated with
     devoted to

3. Depressed
   I feel unhappy
     depressed
     pessimistic
     lost
     miserable
     discouraged
     demoralized
     drained
     terrible
   I feel awful
     lousy
     crummy
     down
     low
     blah
     blue
     down in the dumps

101

4. Inadequate
    I feel incompetent
        inept
        defeated
        overwhelmed
        unsure of myself
        worthless
        powerless
    I feel helpless
        like a failure
    I can't manage
        cope
    I feel trapped
        good for nothing

5. Confused
    I feel undecided
        puzzled
        baffled
        bewildered
        frustrated
        flustered
    I'm in a dilemma
        in a bind
        mixed up
        at loose ends
    I feel like I'm going around in circles

6. Hurt
    I feel degraded
        disgraced
        mistreated
        belittled
        ridiculed
        exploited
        abused
        unappreciated
        taken for granted
    I feel crushed
        destroyed
        wounded
        devastated
        humiliated
        laughed at
        put down
        let down

7. Angry
    I'm dismayed
        annoyed
        agitated
        irritated
        aggravated
        exasperated
        hostile
        upset with
        indignant
    I'm resentful
        bitter
        mad
        disgusted
        furious
        enraged
        outraged
        infuriated
        burned up

8. Lonely
    I feel isolated
        alienated
        ignored
        unwanted
        neglected
        excluded
        distant
    I feel aloof
        lonesome
        left out
        cut off
        worlds apart
        out in the cold

APPENDIX TWO

Expressions to Improve Conversation Skills

1. Asking Questions
2. Asking Follow-Up
3. Hesitating
4. Reporting
5. Paraphrasing
6. Rephrasing
7. Listening Attentively
8. Asking for Repetition
9. Interrupting
10. Returning to the Story
11. Asking for Response
12. Reacting Positively
13. Reacting Negatively
14. Giving Suggestions
15. Accepting Suggestions
16. Turning Down Suggestions
17. Ending a Conversation
18. Thanking
19. Responding to Thanks
20. Leaving

1. Asking Questions
   What's your name?
   Where are you from?
   Where were you born?
   How long have you been in . . .?
   Where do you live now?
   Why did you come to . . .?
   What kind of visa do you have?
   Are you here with your family?

Are you married?
Do you have any children?
When will you return to your country?
Are you eager to return?
Would you prefer to stay here longer?
What do you do for a living?
What's your job like?
What do you enjoy about your job?
What would you like to be doing two years from now? ten years from now?
What are some of your favorite activities here?
What has surprised you about life in this country?
What problems have you run up against here?

2. Asking Follow-Up Questions
    1. *Could you tell me more about* your family?
    2. *Would you mind telling us more about* what happened?
    3. *Something else I'd like to hear about* is your school.
    4. *I'd like to know* why you decided to come here.
    5. *I'd love to hear more about* your parents.
    6. *What else* can you tell us about your school?
    7. *Tell me about it.*

Stronger
Less
Formal

3. Hesitating
    1. Well, . . .
    2. Well, you see . . .
    3. Well, let me think . . .
    4. Let's see now . . .
    5. How shall I put it?
    6. How can I put it?
    7. Mmmmmmmmmmm . . .
    8. Ahhhhhhhhh . . .
    9. That's a good question.
    10. That's an interesting question.
    11. In fact, . . .
    12. The thing is that . . .
    13. I guess that . . .

4. Reporting
    1. *Why did I come?* Well . . .
    2. *You asked me why* I came to the United States.
    3. *You asked me if* I was enjoying my stay here.
    4. *You asked me whether* I would return there soon.
    5. *You wanted to know why* I came here.
    6. *You told us that* you came to study.
    7. *You said that* you were feeling homesick.

5. Paraphrasing
   1. *I think what you're saying is that* you feel lonely.
   2. *If I understand you correctly,* you are really happy here.
   3. *What you want to tell us is that* you were disappointed.
   4. *What you mean is that* you'd like to meet some Americans.
   5. *What you're trying to say is that* you're homesick.
   6. *What you're saying is that* life here is overwhelming.
   7. *In other words,* you like what you see.
   8. *You mean* you want to change your major.

Less Formal

6. Rephrasing
   1. *I'd like to say that* I was surprised when I found out.
   2. *What I want to say is* that you have missed my point.
   3. *What I'm trying to tell you is* how important it is to learn English.
   4. *What I really meant was that* it could have been done.
   5. *I really want to say that* you should have come.
   6. *I'm trying to tell you that* it's unfair.
   7. *I mean that* you could have done it.
   8. *Actually,* I was upset.

Less Formal

7. Listening Attentively

AGREEMENT			
1. Mmm-hmm.	15. Terrific!	28. Oh?	
2. Uh-huh.	16. Wonderful!	29. Oh, really?	
3. Yes.	17. Fantastic!	DISAGREEMENT	
4. Yeah.	SURPRISE	30. Oh, no.	
5. Right.	18. Gee!	31. Uh-uh.	
6. Sure.	19. Oh really?	32. Euh!	
7. I see.	20. What?	33. Impossible!t	
8. I know.	21. Huh?	34. Ridiculous!	
9. Exactly.	22. My goodness!	35. Oh, come on!	
10. I agree.	23. No kidding!	36. No way!	
11. Of course	24. Wow!	37. And then?	
12. Definitely.	DOUBT	CONTINUE	
DELIGHT	25. Maybe.	38. Go on!	
13. Interesting!	26. Well . . .	39. Well?	
14. Great!	27. Hmm.	40. What else?	

8. Asking for Repetition
   1. Would you mind repeating that?
   2. Excuse me, what was that you said?

APPENDIX TWO

   3. Pardon, what did you say?
   4. Could you please repeat that?
   5. I didn't quite follow what you said.
   6. Sorry, what was that?
Informal 7. What?
   8. What was that?
   9. I didn't get that.
   10. I didn't catch what you said.

9. *Interrupting*
  1. Oh, excuse me, but . . .
  2. May I say something?
  3. May I interrupt you for a minute?
  4. I'd like to add something.
  5. I'd just like to say that . . .
  6. Sorry to interrupt you, but . . .
Informal 7. Oh, I just thought of something.
  8. That reminds me . . .
  9. By the way, . . .
  10. Before I forget, . . .

10. Returning to the Story
  1. Well, . . .
  2. Anyway, . . .
  3. As I was saying, . . .
  4. To get back to what I was saying, . . .
  5. To return to the subject, . . .
  6. To return to what I was saying, . . .
  7. Going back to what I said earlier, . . .
  8. Where was I?

11. Asking for Response
  1. What do you think?
  2. How do you feel about that?
  3. Don't you agree?
  4. Isn't that so?
  5. Isn't that true?
  6. Do you know what I mean?

12. Reacting Positively
  1. I agree.
  2. That sounds good.
  3. Good for you!
  4. That's wonderful (great, terrific, fantastic, amazing).
  5. Please go on.

Informal   6. Go on! Tell me more!
                7. Gosh, how fantastic!
                8. Isn't that something?
                9. Wow, that's incredible!
                10. Gee, that's great!
                11. Well, you are really something!
                12. Absolutely, that's it.

13. Reacting Negatively
    1. That may be true, but . . .
    2. I understand what you're saying, but . . .
    3. The problem with that is . . .
    4. Well, I don't really agree.
    5. I'm afraid I disagree.

Very Strong
      6. How could you have?
      7. What made you do that?
      8. Why did you do that?
      9. Oh no, that can't be!
      10. You shouldn't have.
      11. I wish you hadn't.
      12. I don't understand why . . .

14. Giving Suggestions

Polite
    1. Wouldn't it be better if . . .
    2. Wouldn't it be a good idea to . . .

Formal
    3. What I advise you to do is . . .
    4. I suggest that you . . .
    5. I recommend doing that.
    6. Perhaps you could . . .

Less Formal
    7. You can always . . .
    8. Why don't you . . .
    9. How about . . .
    10. Why not . . .
    11. If I were you, I'd . . .

Informal Strong
    12. If I were in your shoes, I'd . . .
    13. You'd better . . .

15. Accepting Suggestions

Hesitant
    1. Perhaps that would work.
    2. Maybe I should try that.
    3. Maybe I'll give that a try.
    4. That sounds like it might work out.

Stronger
    5. I think you've got something there.
    6. Hmm . . . that sounds like a good idea.

Informal

      7. Oh, that's tempting!
      8. Yes, why don't I?
      9. What do you know! Maybe you have something there.

16. Turning Down Suggestions
    1. Is there anything else you can suggest?
    2. Do you have any other ideas?
    3. Is there anything else you would do in my position?
    4. That's not quite what I want.
    5. No, that's not exactly what I had in mind.
    6. I'm not sure that would work.
    7. I think you've misunderstood me.
    8. That doesn't sound too good (interesting, hopeful).
    9. That's not what I need.
    10. I don't see any advantage in doing that.
    11. No, that's no good.
    12. That wouldn't work.

Stronger

17. Ending a Conversation
    1. I'm awfully sorry, but I have to run. I have to catch the five o'clock train.
    2. I'm afraid that I have to go now. Someone is waiting for me downstairs.
    3. Gee, I have an appointment at three o'clock. I have to rush off now.
    4. Oh, it's getting late. I'd better be going.
    5. Well, I think that's about it. I'd better be going. My schedule is really tight.
    6. Oops! Look at the time! I should be going.

Less Formal

18. Thanking
    1. I've really gotten a lot out of this.
    2. I really appreciate your concern (help).
    3. Thanks for your time (advice, help, ideas).
    4. You've really made me think.
    5. Thanks a million (a lot, so much).
    6. It's been good (wonderful, great, terrific) talking with you.
    7. How can I ever thank you enough?
    8. How can I thank you enough for all you've done for me?
    9. You've really been a (great) help.
    10. What a help this has been!
    11. What a relief to get all this off my chest!
    12. Thanks for putting up with me.
    13. I hope I haven't taken up too much of your time.

19. Responding to Thanks
    1. It's been a pleasure talking to you.
    2. It's really been good talking to you.
    3. I've enjoyed talking to you.
    4. I'm glad that you found this helpful.
    5. I'm happy to be of help.
    6. My pleasure.
    7. You're very welcome.
    8. No trouble at all.
    Often a person offers more help when thanked.
    9. Let me know if I can be of any more help.
    10. Let me know how things work out.
    11. Keep in touch.
20. Leaving
    1. See you.
    2. See you soon.
    3. Let's get together again soon.
    4. Do call.
    5. Give me a call.
    6. How about dinner next week?
    7. Let me know when you're free.
    8. How about getting together for lunch?
    9. How about having a drink next week?
    10. Let me know how you're doing.
    11. Maybe we can get together again soon.
    12. If you're ever in the neighborhood, drop by.
    13. Take care.
    14. Take it easy.

Responses
    15. Sounds great!
    16. Terrific!
    17. Okay. I'll let you know when I'm free.
    18. See you later.
    19. I'll call you next week.
    20. Sure, sounds good.

Oral Histories

Dear Student:

Here are some hints on how to prepare to be a mystery student.

1. Read the story that you have been assigned several times, until you feel comfortable with the information presented.
2. Ask yourself these questions:
   - What is the person like?
   - What are his/her joys and sorrows?
   - What is his/her environment like?
   - What is his/her daily life like?
3. If these questions are not answered in the story, feel free to imagine the missing pieces of this person's life.
4. Discuss your ideas about the mystery student with the other students assigned to be the same character.
5. The goal is not to memorize, but to create a person based on some of the facts presented in the oral history.
6. You will want to study and think about the meanings of the italicized words and phrases. They may be new to you.
7. You will find ways to help you express yourself as the mystery student in the lists in Appendix 2, page 103.

Yoko Hiyakawa's Story (Chapter 3)

My name is Yoko Hiyakawa. When I was twenty-five and still unmarried, I decided to come to the United States. I did not want an arranged marriage and I had not yet found a husband *on my own.* I felt *trapped* at my parents' house and like a failure whenever I visited any of my girlfriends. They were all married, and were either pregnant or already had children. Each one was working on her "two-child" family. I felt I no longer had a place in the society. When I heard my bank was transferring some employees to the United States, I *grabbed at* the chance to relocate.

Now it's been four years since I arrived. I don't feel *left out* here; I have my own apartment and have seen many single women like me living here. Yet in my apartment I sometimes feel *isolated* because I find it difficult to invite people over. I guess I'm not *used to doing* it. And at work I feel *frustrated.* I see young men called "trainees" given *prestigious* titles and interesting work although I have been at the bank far longer than they have. I have *the same* college education *as* they have. My duties seem to vary from xeroxing to making tea. Soon I fear that I will not even be doing that because these male office workers like to see young pretty faces and I'm getting past that pleasing stage.

If I *speak up* at work, I feel I will be viewed as *too aggressive.* I feel *jealous of* these young *know-nothings* who are *moving up the ladder* and leaving me behind. My English isn't good enough to try my luck at an American company. Also, I don't think I'm direct enough to work with Americans. I think they would misunderstand my smiles.

Jaime Gonzalez's Story (Chapter 4)

My name is Jaime Gonzalez and you can almost always find me somewhere in my neighborhood, around 9th Avenue and 22nd Street. I'm the super[1] of the big building on the corner, the twelve-story one next to the *bodega*.[2] I dream of passing the Post Office exam and of becoming a mail carrier. It looks like a good job for me: good pay, great *benefits* and job security. I finished high school in Puerto Rico and I learned some English there. But twice I've *failed* the Post Office exam. I'm going to try again next year.

Meanwhile, I have to *deal with* everyone complaining in the building. Some say there's too much heat; others say there's not enough. And most of my tenants say it's an emergency when it isn't. Last week, when the *boiler broke down,* we almost had a *rent strike.* But usually the building runs *pretty* smoothly.

My biggest problem is my wife. She spends her day at home watching Spanish television. Since our children *moved out,* she's been *bored.* I have a lot of *buddies* I play *dominos* with and drink with on the corner. But she sits alone in the apartment. I know there's not much excitement in her life. Her English is so poor that she doesn't even understand when the neighbors try to make conversation with her on the elevator. This morning I heard one neighbor say, "Where are you going, Mrs. Gonzalez?" My wife answered, "Fine, thanks. How are you?"

My wife asked me if I would pay for an English course for her. I'd like her to go, but I just don't know where to send her. Besides, I don't think I could *afford* it. I'm spending more than $8,000 a year on my daughter so that she can become a medical technician. And you know a super doesn't make that much money.

[1]super—superintendent, a handyman in a building
[2]*bodega*—small grocery store in a Spanish-speaking neighborhood

Jeong-Ja Kim's Story (Chapter 5)

I run around carrying trays *loaded down* with dirty dishes, but I *used to be* a classical Korean dancer. In fact, seven years ago I came here with my dance company and performed all over the United States. I could have returned to Korea, but the variety of faces on the streets and the thought of making money were too exciting. After I decided to stay, though, the only dance job I could get was at a Korean night club. It was *degrading*. I no longer felt like a professional. I *couldn't stand it*. Since I could *barely* speak a word of English, the only other job I could find was as a waitress at a Korean restaurant. The hours are long and the work is hard. But it is much better than dancing for *a bunch of* drunks.

Then my tourist visa *expired*. I was afraid of staying here illegally. I decided to pay an American man to marry me so that I could get a green card. Many of my friends have done that. It did upset me to marry that way because I knew I could never tell my parents. But there was no other solution to be legal. I found a man who charged me $5,000.

Since then, I have fallen in love with the cook at my restaurant. He's Korean and has no papers either. We have decided to live together without being married. Because *I'm married to* the American, we had no choice. This is very unusual for someone from my country to do.

I feel a little bit *scared of* what I'm doing. Some of the *busboys* at the restaurant have warned me: "Watch out! That cook is lazy and he loves to gamble in Atlantic City.[1]" But I think he's a good man. Of course, I can't let my mother know that I'm living with him. She's quite a religious Christian and wouldn't understand.

When I do get my green card, save some money, and learn more English, I'm going to try to open up my own business. Maybe I'll sell make-up. Maybe I'll work with my friends at a vegetable store. Then I'll *get divorced* so I can marry the cook.

---

[1] Atlantic City—A city in New Jersey famous for its gambling casinos.

Gerard Le Pont's Story (Chapter 6)

My name is Gerard Le Pont. When I first arrived in the United States, I hadn't planned to stay. All I had thought I would do was to study hotel management at Cornell University in Ithaca, New York. But I *fell in love with* an American woman. My parents were *delighted* when they heard I was *settling down* with a nice young woman—"my piano teacher," I told them. But when I brought her home at Christmas, they were *shocked*.

The woman I love is black and is eight years older than I am. My parents were very *broad-minded* about having an American as a daughter-in-law. In fact, I think they enjoyed *chatting* with neighbors about the new American addition to their family.

My parents live in the *suburbs* outside of Paris and their neighbors *envy* the life style on "Dallas."[1] They equate Hollywood with America. So of course they envied my mother's position, imagining that my mother was a little bit closer to Hollywood. However, when my fiancé and I arrived in my small village, I could feel the *stares* of the neighbors. All were *lined up* at their windows, *peering down* at us from behind the curtains. They were probably *chuckling* to themselves that instead of bringing my mother Hollywood, I had brought her Harlem—the *ghetto*.

My parents never mentioned her color, although I am quite sure it was her color that distressed them. Instead, they kept saying, "When you're forty-two, she'll be fifty. When you're forty-nine, she'll almost be sixty." I would reply, "But women live longer than men. When she's eighty, I'll probably be dead." My mother would bite her lips *repressing* whatever else she wanted to say. That's when I decided that I wanted to live in America, far from my disapproving parents.

[1]"Dallas"—a popular television show whose main characters are wealthy Texans.

Dina Rubinov's Story (Chapter 7)

Being a chemical engineer with *a poor command* of English did not *land me* a job very quickly when I arrived in this country from Russia. The job market was *in a slump;* my twenty years of experience did not count much. After sending out 400 *résumés* and receiving not one positive response, I decided that it was time to change careers, even at the late age of forty-five. That's when I saw the need to go back to school. Where was the job market headed? I thought it was computer science, but I'm not sure what would be the best field to study now. In Russia, I was *guaranteed* work, so there was never an opportunity to change professions. In Russia, I couldn't advance much at my company because I was a Jew.

My present *dilemma* is whether or not to raise my child as a Jew[1] in this country. I left Russia with thousands of other Jews because of religious *persecution.* We were told that Judaism was our nationality; it was even stamped on our passports. When I came to this country, I found that many orthodox Jews didn't consider me a real Jew because I had never been to a synagogue and because I had little interest in practicing the religion.

At first, I sent my five-year-old daughter to a yeshiva[2] because I thought that was where she belonged. But then she started coming home accusing us, her parents, of not being real Jews because we didn't keep a kosher[3] house or light candles on Friday nights and my husband didn't wear a *yarmulke.*[4] I decided that this was *similar to* the persecution I had felt in Russia.

Now my child goes to public school. I think she should decide for herself if she wants to be a Jew and what being a Jew means to her. She's ten now. I'm so *proud of* her. She did not speak a word of English until she was five. I used to have to *struggle* in my broken English to explain to the teacher why my daughter was late or absent. Now she does all of the explaining herself. In fact, she just won a city-wide storytelling contest. Among the five winners, she was the only foreign-born student. Isn't that something? Imagine—there's not *a trace of* accent in her English. Lucky girl, I say. I'll never lose mine.

[1] Jew—2 percent of Americans are Jewish. There are three main divisions among Jews: orthodox (the most religious), conservative and reformed.
[2] yeshiva—a Jewish school.
[3] kosher—fulfilling the requirements of Jewish dietary law.
[4] *yarmulke*—a small cap worn by religious Jewish men as a sign of reverence.

Hector Rodriguez's Story (Chapter 8)

My name is Hector Rodriguez. I *floated* in *an inner tube* across the Rio Grande to come to America. It cost me $350 to be *smuggled across* the border to Texas. That was three years ago. Since then, I've paid this *smuggler* almost a thousand dollars to bring my wife and three children.

An American might not understand why I had to leave Mexico. Sometimes I don't understand. At times we were hungry in Mexico, but I've found out that the roads are not *paved with gold* here either. I think that's just some *fable made up* by dreamers. Yes, I have a television, a radio cassette player, and a refrigerator taller than my wife. But the five of us have to live in this *cramped* apartment. And I'm working two jobs for this!

During the day I work as a janitor. When I work overtime, I sometimes arrive late at my night job in a parking lot. Despite my two jobs, my wife, who works as a maid, often brings home more money than I do. The people she works for give her big tips almost every week. It really makes me uncomfortable to have her be the bigger *wage earner.* She doesn't even know as much English as I do! *I'd rather* she stay home with the kids as she did in Mexico. But I can't afford not to have her work.

What is most important now is for us to become legal residents. A friend tells me that I can buy *false* papers. I'm afraid of doing that. I'm afraid of being *deported.* I think that with papers I could get a better job, medical insurance—all the things I dreamed of having when I was in Mexico. I just don't know what's going to happen to us. Will the American dream come true for my children?

May Chang's Story (Chapter 9)

Did you know that my mother and father have been here for fifteen years and can *hardly carry on* a simple conversation in English? I'm twenty-one and my name is May Chang. Ever since I was little, I've been acting as a translator for my parents. When I was eight years old and *barely* tall enough to reach the wall phone, I can remember calling the telephone company for my parents about some error on a bill. In fact, I *rarely* have a peaceful hour to myself when I'm home. My mom will *stare at* the television when I watch my favorite program. As the story *rolls on,* she will ask, "And what did he say to her? And what did she answer? And what . . ."

Both of my parents work in a factory. They sew all day long, next to other Taiwanese immigrants. I *feel bad for* them. I see how they struggle to *make ends meet* and save so that I can attend New York University. But as much as I love them, *I wish they would* become more *Americanized* or understand my *Americanization.* "A Chinese girl lives with her parents until she marries." My mother repeats this whenever I mention the possibility of getting a place of my own. My American friends live such free lives, dating and staying out late. I envy them.

This year I'll *graduate with a major in* math. When I get a job, I'll try to *change her mind* and move out. I'm getting *tired of* apologizing to my friends about not being able to join them. But I worry about my parents. Who will translate my favorite television programs for them? Will they ever understand that a twenty-one-year-old woman would want to live on her own?

Taeb Omar's Story (Chapter 10)

You might not believe this, but the owner of the All-American Fried Chicken restaurant is me, Taeb Omar, a thirty-five-year-old political refugee from Afghanistan. You might ask, "What could you know about American fried chicken?" Well, after tasting Kentucky fried chicken, I knew I could make the bird even *tastier* by adding some of my native *spices,* like *garlic* and hot pepper. It's been three years since I opened my first chicken *outlet.* I feel like I can't open enough of them. Because both men and women work in America, nobody has time to cook dinner anymore. So everybody needs a wife. I'm everybody's wife. The line forms at five P.M. at the *take-out* counter with these *tired-out,* hungry workers. For me, America has been a land of opportunity.

You may see my Buick Skylark and my *two-family* house and think I came here to make money. But I didn't come here for money. It was my mother and my sister who wanted me to leave Afghanistan. I was about to leave for Russia to learn how to be a pilot. I wasn't against going. But my mother swore that *no son of hers* would be *drafted.* She saved money with my older sister and sent me to West Germany. I wasn't *getting ahead* there, so I came to the States.

I don't like to tell people I'm a *draft dodger.* For most people this word has a terrible meaning. But I'm not a *coward* or *unpatriotic.* I love my country and the people. I'm sad I can't go back now to visit. I just wish my mother and sister could come here and taste my chicken.

Heidi Tobler's Story (Chapter 11)

In Switzerland, my father is a *successful butcher* who cannot understand why I didn't want to work in the butcher shop and why I wanted to come to the United States to study *art therapy.* In the shop, my brother kills the cows, my mother serves the customers, my sister keeps the books, and I was expected to make the sausage. My father *might have understood* if I had wanted to be a teacher or an architect, but an art therapist was too foreign for him. Since my father didn't *approve of* my coming to the States to study art therapy, my mother sends me Swiss francs secretly through the mail to help me pay for my graduate studies.

After a year here, both my mother and father came to see what *I was up to.* I live in a good neighborhood, but in an old building. After climbing five *flights of stairs* in an unlit hallway, they entered my apartment. It was *crawling with cockroaches,* and my parents were *flabbergasted.* I had left beautiful, modern, clean Switzerland for this? They thought I had *lost my mind.* Did I want to live in a country where people don't take proper care of their property?

They noticed the garbage *piled high* in front of my building. They didn't seem to *appreciate* that no one *on the block* cared that they were here. But that's what I really love about living here. I have a real *sense of privacy* I never had before. At home in Matzigen, when I bought a double bed, all the neighbors' *tongues were wagging,* wondering if I had found myself a male friend. At home in Matzigen, when I came home late, the next morning my neighbor would inform me of how many times my phone had rung while I was out. I felt I couldn't *breathe* without someone recording how fast my heartbeat was. Any friend I brought home was inspected. Any *dent* in my car was noticed. But here my neighbors don't even know my name and don't care about whom I invite home. What a paradise!

Ali Fahrid's Story (Chapter 12)

I got four hours of sleep last night because I'm the night watchman at a big midtown hotel. That's my usual schedule because during the day I'm *drilling* teeth at New York University Dental School. You see, I'm actually an Egyptian dentist. I never touched a pair of *handcuffs* or a *blackjack* before I came here. But when I arrived, the American Dental Association said I needed to go back to school for two years before they would let me practice. It didn't matter to them that I had been practicing in Egypt for more than four years. So here I am, a student again. I feel a bit *anxious* that I will be thirty by the time I get started *building up* my career. But what am I doing working at the hotel at nights? The *fees* at dental school are *exorbitant*. In Egypt, school was free. Anyway, I have to pay those bills. That's why I have to work at the hotel.

On my job at the hotel, I am *supposed to* make sure that nobody steals the customers' baggage or picks their pockets. It's a very uncomfortable position to be in. If a man is *hanging around* the lobby, I'm supposed to ask him what he is doing there. You can always make mistakes. Once I stopped a man wearing old blue jeans. But the luggage he was carrying *turned out* to be his own. I've had to learn how to apologize very well in English. Another time I caught a *rather well-dressed* man walking off with someone else's bag. In America it's certainly hard to tell who's who by his dress. *Little did I expect* these types of problems when I decided to be a dentist here. *I'd much rather be* drilling teeth *than* handcuffing thieves!

Alejandra Maldonado's Story (Chapter 13)

I'm tired of hearing Americans say, "Alejandra Maldonado, you're from Colómbia. Do you smoke *marijuana?*" The *stereotype* that people have of my countrymen is that we are always busy *trafficking in drugs* and that if we are not *involved in* smuggling marijuana, then we certainly must be users. They picture a Colómbian woman with a joint[1] *hanging out of* her mouth as she dances the *cumbia*[2] in a tight skirt with very high heels. Americans simply can't believe that I have never tried marijuana and that I can't even dance. What I am is a graduate student studying social work. What I have been doing lately is running around in my *jogging* shoes to try to find a good place to live.

Before arriving here, I never realized how *severe* the apartment *shortage* was in New York City. I get up at six-thirty in the morning on Wednesdays and wait for the *Village Voice*[3] to be delivered so I can read the new ads for available apartments. I circle the ads that sound good, and I rush to a pay telephone, my pocket filled with quarters. I usually get a busy signal or an answering machine. Last week I finally found a beautifully *renovated* studio on the fifth floor of a *walk-up facing a* garden. Since I was the first to see the apartment, I was sure it was mine. But the superintendent seemed *reluctant* to give it to me. At first, I thought he wanted some money *under the table.* Then I thought he didn't like me because I was Hispanic.[4] It *turned out* that what disturbed him was my three-year-old *German shepherd.* "I'll give you that apartment right away if you *get rid of* that dog," he said. I was *amazed.* I had thought that Americans were the dog lovers of the world: hundreds of varieties of dogfood on supermarket shelves, dog cemeteries, dog restaurants, and even dog psychiatrists!

Anyway, I am not about to *give up* my dog. Perhaps I should put an ad in the paper saying "American-born German shepherd and nonsmoking Colómbian woman looking for studio to rent."

[1]joint—a marijuana cigarette.
[2]*cumbia*—a popular dance from the north of Colómbia.
[3]*Village Voice*—a weekly newspaper in New York City that has many classified ads.
[4]Hispanic—a person of Spanish heritage.

Stanley Wolinski's Story (Chapter 14)

Everyone who takes my cab guesses that I'm from Eastern Europe. I can't *get rid of* this Polish accent. Last year I bought a tape recorder and worked with *a private tutor*. But every week we talked about the same errors. I forgot my articles; I used the wrong preposition; I pronounced "g" too strongly at the end of words. After three months, I *gave up*. It was too *frustrating*; besides, I can *make myself understood*.

You see, in my country I was considered a bright guy. I was a translator from Russian into Polish. So what am I doing in a cab, you may ask. It's good money and I'm my own boss. And here there isn't much need for a Russian–Polish translator.

Although when I first came here, I worked as a doorman at the Hyatt Regency. But I was more than just a doorman. They gave me the title of "doorman/translator." When there were guests from Russia or Poland, I had the pleasure of telling them about the United States, suggesting where to go and where not to go. But most of the time I was just a regular doorman. People never got to talk to me to find out who I really was. That's why being in a cab is *more rewarding*. I really get to talk to people.

I didn't come to this country to drive a cab. The real reason I am here is for my sixteen-year-old son. I thought he would have a better future here. But now I am worried about the education he's been getting in public school. He is doing multiplication here, while in Poland he was finished with algebra. It all seems too easy. Teachers aren't *strict enough* with him. They accept the *sloppiest* homework. I really think that he *gets away with murder* in school. I want him to be a *white-collar worker*—a doctor, a lawyer, or a future senator.

Do you know what he told me yesterday? "Pa, I want to be a rock star." How am I ever going to convince him to go to college? *After all,* I came to the States so he could become anything he wanted, but not a rock star!

Marie Lionne's Story (Chapter 15)

When my boyfriend told me that he had to return to Haiti, he promised me he would be back soon to marry me. Two months passed without a word from him. I wasn't sure about what I should do. I decided I couldn't wait forever for him and started dating again. Nineteen was too young to give up on men! Some friends told me that he did come back to the United States and *became enraged* when he found out I was seeing other men. I feel very hurt that he didn't even call me. But I don't think that I *would have married* him. He was too *bossy* and too jealous.

Maybe I'm too *picky* about men. But since being here I've learned that being an independent woman isn't impossible. I *can't take it* if a man is stupidly jealous. A little jealousy is healthy, but too much would *drive me up a wall*. Also, I don't want to be with a man who is *overpowering*, who feels that he is the master. I understand that I will have to *compromise* a bit but not as much as my mother has had to. Yes, that's one thing I'm going to have *to cope with* better—my father. Here I can come back to the dormitory at any time. But in Haiti my father says that if I'm home one minute after ten, *he'll kill me*. But I never lie, so he should trust me.

Despite this time problem at home, I want to go back and serve my country. They need good teachers. My work will have so much more meaning there than here. I'm not going to be part of the *brain drain*.

Koji Watanabe's Story (Chapter 16)

My wife had a baby boy last month and I won't get to see her or my son for a year. I'm Koji Watanabe, a trainee at Toyomenka. The boss has decided that we trainees will *devote ourselves* more *to* our work and to our study of American management skills if we are not *distracted by* our Japanese wives and children. But I feel *at loose ends* without my family. I've never been on my own. I never even learned how to cook. And whom can I discuss my reaction to America with?

What first disturbed me about America is that Americans are always busy eating. My American secretary has a supply of cookies, gum and candy to last her through the day so that her mouth is never empty, not even when she's speaking on the phone. Even on the streets, Americans seem to be constantly *snacking,* whether they're *licking* ice cream cones or *munching on* hot dogs. In the evening course I'm taking in management the students eat pizza and drink coffee during the class. The professor drinks and smokes while he lectures. Yet right above his head hangs a sign that says, "No smoking or eating in this room." Why are Americans always eating? I think it's *unhealthy.* Maybe that's why there are so many fat people here.

I was also surprised when I went to the Wall Street Racquet Club and somebody stole the change out of my pants pocket while I was in the shower. I was really *shocked* that this could have happened in a private club! I feel like I can't trust other people. I had to borrow some money from my tennis partner so that I could get home. It was very *embarrassing* to have to ask for money from this American businessman whom I hardly knew and whom I had just beaten in tennis. He, fortunately, was very kind and *insisted* on lending me more than I really needed. I think I've learned my lesson about being more careful; but I haven't learned how to feel happy living alone.

Kenny Lee's Story (Chapter 17)

When I went back to Hong Kong for summer vacation, I realized how much one year of graduate school in the United States had changed me. I felt like a foreigner in my own hometown. On the streets there was no variety of faces. I saw everything with different eyes. To visit a family of six all sleeping in one room seemed *shocking.* I hadn't realized until then how quickly I had gained the critical eyes of a traveler. When I finish my Ph.D. in computer science and return home, I wonder if I will *become numb* to those sights as I was before. But I really understand now how travel makes a man; I just feel so much older and wiser than before.

Now the new semester has begun again at Boston University. Students are back in the dormitory. And tonight an old Woody Allen film *is being shown* at the student center. I *used to think* he was funny when his films were *dubbed* in Chinese. But understanding American humor seems impossible. It's uncomfortable sitting in a movie theater, listening to the *roars of laughter* and sitting there quietly. I hear the words. I just don't *get the jokes.* In fact, the whole idea of joking seems so American. Even Presidents begin their speeches with a little joke. My American roommate told me that a good joke was a way to *loosen up* an audience. I'd like to have that power. Maybe tonight at the movies I'll learn one. My roommate promised to *act as a* translator for me tonight. Aren't I lucky?

José Ojeda's Story (Chapter 18)

When I first arrived in New York from Caracas, Venezuela, I *followed my friend's advice* and got a *drive-away car* that had to be delivered to San Francisco in four days. What a dream—a free car to drive across America! I needed to be in Berkeley by September 9th to start my master's degree in counseling psychology, so I had time to explore the United States. I drove from Manhattan to San Francisco and *not once was I stopped* by a policeman nor was I asked for identification. In Venezuela, the police are always *hassling* you for papers wherever you travel. I really appreciate that freedom.

Yes, living here is easy. The phones work! I couldn't believe it when I *got back* a quarter that I had lost in a public phone. The mail works! I was so used to Venezuela, where I had to pay all my bills *in person* because the mail just couldn't be trusted. I have much more time here.

Yet with all this freedom and convenience, my money is *shrinking.* The Venezuelan bolivar has really *gone down.* When I translate how much I pay for tuition, food, or a dentist into bolivars, my parents go crazy. I'm thinking of getting a part-time job next semester. There was an ad about an older woman in a *wheelchair* who wanted a companion some afternoons. That way I could practice English and *ease the strain* on my parents' finances.